STEAMPUNK
POE

BY EDGAR ALLAN POE

ILLUSTRATED BY ZDENKO BASIC AND MANUEL SUMBERAC

RP | TEENS
PHILADELPHIA • LONDON

Books published by Running Press are available at special discounts for bulk
purchases in the United States by corporations, institutions, and other organizations.
For more information, please contact the Special Markets Department at
the Perseus Books Group, 2300 Chestnut Street, Suite 200, Philadelphia, PA 19103,
or call (800) 810-4145, ext. 5000, or e-mail special.markets@perseusbooks.com.

ISBN 978-0-7624-4192-1
Library of Congress Control Number: 2011923362

E-book ISBN 978-0-7624-4387-1

9 8 7 6 5 4 3 2 1
Digit on the right indicates the number of this printing

Cover and interior design by Frances J. Soo Ping Chow
Edited by Ellie O'Ryan and Marlo Scrimizzi
Typography: Phaeton and Requiem

Published by Running Press Teens
an imprint of Running Press Book Publishers
A Member of the Perseus Books Group
2300 Chestnut Street
Philadelphia, PA 19103–4371

Visit us on the web!
www.runningpress.com

TABLE OF CONTENTS

I. STORIES

II. POEMS

Introduction

The steampunk genre didn't exist when Edgar Allan Poe was penning his masterful mysteries and nightmarish horror stories, so you might be wondering how, exactly, the two have come together in this book. The greatest writers, though, produce works that transcend their own times, allowing each new generation of readers to discover them anew. And Edgar Allan Poe is nothing if not one of the greatest American writers in history.

But to understand exactly how well Edgar and steampunk go together, it might be helpful to know a little about Edgar himself—and what inspired him to write the way he did.

Edgar Poe was born on January 19, 1809, in Boston, Massachusetts. His early life was cloaked in much of the mystery and heartbreak that is woven through the canon of his works. Not long after Edgar was born, his father disappeared, abandoning the family; Edgar's mother died shortly thereafter. Young Edgar was then taken in by John and Frances Allan, a wealthy family from Richmond, Virginia; though they never formally adopted him, their surname became his middle, creating a name that would earn a place in the annals of great American writers.

Edgar had a tumultuous relationship with his foster father, but that did not interfere with John's plans for Edgar's education, including a boarding school in England and enrollment in the newly-formed University of Virginia. Edgar, however, was soon expelled for debauchery that included drinking and gambling, leading to an even greater rift with John. Frances died in 1829, leaving Edgar motherless again. To honor her deathbed wish, Edgar and John tried to mend their relationship, but the reconciliation was short-lived. Despite the bad feelings between the two, Edgar never dropped the "Allan" from his name—even after John eventually disowned him.

Determined to seek his fortune as a writer from an early age, Edgar returned to his hometown of Boston, where his first collection of poems, *Tamerlane*, was published when he was just 18 years old. Though these poems were anonymously credited to "A Bostonian," Edgar was surely disappointed when his first foray into publication was met with virtually no attention. A stint in the Army, followed by enrollment at the United States Military Academy in West Point, New York, offered a similar outcome to his time at the University of Virginia.

Edgar, however, was undaunted in pursuit of publication. In 1835, at the age of 26, he married his 13-year-old cousin, Virginia Clem, and moved to Fordham, New York. There Edgar made a name for himself not as a writer of original works, but as a keen literary critic, which earned him many enemies among his contemporaries. Still, with dogged determination, Edgar continued to write dozens of short stories and poems that explored his fascination with mysteries, puzzles, death, and the macabre. Especially after the death of Virginia in 1847, Edgar's poems were fraught with a recurring theme of the untimely death of a beautiful young woman—echoing, perhaps, Edgar's own personal tragedies: the death of his mother, his foster mother, and his beloved wife. He was well-regarded among his friends and many luminaries of the literary world, despite how frequently Edgar required financial rescuing from various debts and debacles.

Poe's own untimely death, at age 40, is shrouded in a mystery that perhaps only his great detective character, C. Auguste Dupin, could solve. On October 3, 1849, Edgar was found covered in filth, ill, virtually incoherent—and, strangely enough, wearing clothes that did not belong to him. Though Edgar was immediately hospitalized, he never recovered, and indeed was unable to explain the bizarre circumstances that had brought him to such a sorry state of affairs. After Edgar's death, several theories circulated as to the cause of his demise, including cholera, tuberculosis, alcoholism, and even rabies. It is now known that one of his most bitter literary enemies, Rufus Wilmot Griswold, worked tirelessly after Edgar's death to discredit him by spreading false rumors that Edgar died of drug addiction, as well as penning a hateful obituary and a biography studded with brazen lies.

So many years after he left this earth, what remains most important is Edgar's literary legacy: poems and stories that still chill and thrill with their horrifying descriptions and shocking twists, all wrapped up in evocative word choices that delight generation after generation of readers. He originated the detective story (beginning with *The Murders in the Rue Morgue*, *The Mystery of Marie Rogêt*, and *The Purloined Letter*), and entire genres like science fiction benefited from Edgar's unparalleled talent. The steampunk genre, which currently enjoys immense popularity, was decades away from invention when Edgar was writing; yet it's clear how many of his stories and poems provide an essential framework for it. From Edgar's interest in technological advancements like hot-air balloons in *The Balloon Hoax* to his elaborate descriptions of ornate architecture and lavish fashion in *The Fall of the House of Usher*, *The Spectacles*, and *The Masque of the Red Death*, the many charms of steampunk also serve as hallmarks of his writing. And, certainly, Edgar's assorted cast of murderers and madmen offer an opportunity to explore some of the steampunk movement's darker, more disturbing components. Whatever silent secrets about his life and death lie buried with him in a grave at Westminster Hall and Burying Grounds in Maryland, Edgar Allan Poe's body of work continues to speak for itself.

1. STORIES

The Masque of the Red Death

THE "Red Death" had long devastated the country. No pestilence had ever been so fatal, or so hideous. Blood was its Avatar and its seal—the redness and the horror of blood. There were sharp pains, and sudden dizziness, and then profuse bleeding at the pores, with dissolution. The scarlet stains upon the body and especially upon the face of the victim, were the pest ban which shut him out from the aid and from the sympathy of his fellow-men. And the whole seizure, progress, and termination of the disease, were the incidents of half an hour.

But the Prince Prospero was happy and dauntless and sagacious. When his dominions were half depopulated, he summoned to his presence a thousand hale and light-hearted friends from among the knights and dames of his court, and with these retired to the deep seclusion of one of his castellated abbeys. This was an extensive and magnificent structure, the creation of the prince's own eccentric yet august taste. A strong and lofty wall girdled it in. This wall had gates of iron. The courtiers, having entered, brought furnaces and massy hammers and welded the bolts. They resolved to leave means neither of ingress nor egress to the sudden impulses of despair or of frenzy from within. The abbey was amply provisioned. With such precautions the courtiers might bid defiance to contagion. The external world could take care of itself. In the meantime it was folly to grieve, or to think. The prince had provided all the appliances of pleasure. There were buffoons, there were improvisatori, there were ballet-dancers, there were musicians, there was Beauty, there was wine. All these and security were within. Without was the "Red Death."

It was toward the close of the fifth or sixth month of his seclusion, and while the pestilence raged most furiously abroad, that the Prince Prospero entertained his thousand friends at a masked ball of the most unusual magnificence.

It was a voluptuous scene, that masquerade. But first let me tell of the rooms in which it was held. These were seven—an imperial suite. In many palaces, however, such suites form a long and straight vista, while the folding doors slide back nearly to the walls on either hand, so that the view of the whole extent is scarcely impeded. Here the case was very different; as might have been expected from the duke's love of the *bizarre*. The apartments were so irregularly disposed that the

vision embraced but little more than one at a time. There was a sharp turn at every twenty or thirty yards, and at each turn a novel effect. To the right and left, in the middle of each wall, a tall and narrow Gothic window looked out upon a closed corridor which pursued the windings of the suite. These windows were of stained glass whose color varied in accordance with the prevailing hue of the decorations of the chamber into which it opened. That at the eastern extremity was hung, for example in blue—and vividly blue were its windows. The second chamber was purple in its ornaments and tapestries, and here the panes were purple. The third was green throughout, and so were the casements. The fourth was furnished and lighted with orange—the fifth with white—the sixth with violet. The seventh apartment was closely shrouded in black velvet tapestries that hung all over the ceiling and down the walls, falling in heavy folds upon a carpet of the same material and hue. But in this chamber only, the color of the windows failed to correspond with the decorations. The panes here were scarlet—a deep blood color. Now in no one of the seven apartments was there any lamp or candelabrum, amid the profusion of golden ornaments that lay scattered to and fro or depended from the roof. There was no light of any kind emanating from lamp or candle within the suite of chambers. But in the corridors that followed the suite, there stood, opposite to each window, a heavy tripod, bearing a brazier of fire, that projected its rays through the tinted glass and so glaringly illumined the room. And thus were produced a multitude of gaudy and fantastic appearances. But in the western or black chamber the effect of the fire-light that streamed upon the dark hangings through the blood-tinted panes was ghastly in the extreme, and produced so wild a look upon the countenances of those who entered, that there were few of the company bold enough to set foot within its precincts at all.

It was in this apartment, also, that there stood against the western wall, a gigantic clock of ebony. Its pendulum swung to and fro with a dull, heavy, monotonous clang; and when the minute-hand made the circuit of the face, and the hour was to be stricken, there came from the brazen lungs of the clock a sound which was clear and loud and deep and exceedingly musical, but of so peculiar a note and emphasis that, at each lapse of an hour, the musicians of the orchestra were constrained to pause, momentarily, in their performance, to hearken to the sound; and thus the waltzers perforce ceased their evolutions; and there was a brief disconcert of the whole gay company; and, while the chimes of the clock yet rang, it was observed that the giddiest grew pale, and the more aged and sedate passed their hands over their brows as if in confused revery or meditation. But when the echoes had fully ceased, a light laughter at once pervaded the assembly;

the musicians looked at each other and smiled as if at their own nervousness and folly, and made whispering vows, each to the other, that the next chiming of the clock should produce in them no similar emotion; and then, after the lapse of sixty minutes (which embrace three thousand and six hundred seconds of the Time that flies), there came yet another chiming of the clock, and then were the same disconcert and tremulousness and meditation as before.

But, in spite of these things, it was a gay and magnificent revel. The tastes of the duke were peculiar. He had a fine eye for colors and effects. He disregarded the *decora* of mere fashion. His plans were bold and fiery, and his conceptions glowed with barbaric lustre. There are some who would have thought him mad. His followers felt that he was not. It was necessary to hear and see and touch him to be *sure* that he was not.

He had directed, in great part, the movable embellishments of the seven chambers, upon occasion of this great *fête*; and it was his own guiding taste which had given character to the masqueraders. Be sure they were grotesque. There were much glare and glitter and piquancy and phantasm—much of what has been since seen in "Hernani." There were arabesque figures with unsuited limbs and appointments. There were delirious fancies such as the madman fashions. There were much of the beautiful, much of the wanton, much of the *bizarre*, something of the terrible, and not a little of that which might have excited disgust. To and fro in the seven chambers there stalked, in fact, a multitude of dreams. And these— the dreams—writhed in and about, taking hue from the rooms, and causing the wild music of the orchestra to seem as the echo of their steps. And, anon, there strikes the ebony clock which stands in the hall of the velvet. And then, for a moment, all is still, and all is silent save the voice of the clock. The dreams are stiff-frozen as they stand. But the echoes of the chime die away—they have endured but an instant—and a light, half-subdued laughter floats after them as they depart. And now again the music swells, and the dreams live, and writhe to and fro more merrily than ever, taking hue from the many-tinted windows through which stream the rays from the tripods. But to the chamber which lies most westwardly of the seven there are now none of the maskers who venture; for the night is waning away; and there flows a ruddier light through the blood-colored panes; and the blackness of the sable drapery appals; and to him whose foot falls upon the sable carpet, there comes from the near clock of ebony a muf-fled peal more solemnly emphatic than any which reaches *their* ears who indulge in the more remote gaieties of the other apartments.

But these other apartments were densely crowded, and in them beat fever-ishly the heart of life. And the revel went whirlingly on, until at length there commenced the sounding of midnight upon the clock. And then the music

ceased, as I have told; and the evolutions of the waltzers were quieted; and there

was an uneasy cessation of all things as before. But now there were twelve strokes

to be sounded by the bell of the clock; and thus it happened, perhaps, that more

of thought crept, with more of time, into the meditations of the thoughtful

among those who revelled. And thus too, it happened, perhaps, that before the

last echoes of the last chime had utterly sunk into silence, there were many indi-

viduals in the crowd who had found leisure to become aware of the presence of

a masked figure which had arrested the attention of no single individual before.

And the rumour of this new presence having spread itself whisperingly around,

there arose at length from the whole company a buzz, or murmur, expressive of

disapprobation and surprise—then, finally, of terror, of horror, and of disgust.

In an assembly of phantasms such as I have painted, it may well be supposed

that no ordinary appearance could have excited such sensation. In truth the

masquerade license of the night was nearly unlimited; but the figure in question

had out-Heroded Herod, and gone beyond the bounds of even the prince's

indefinite decorum. There are chords in the hearts of the most reckless which

cannot be touched without emotion. Even with the utterly lost, to whom life and

death are equally jests, there are matters of which no jest can be made. The

whole company, indeed, seemed now deeply to feel that in the costume and bearing of the stranger neither wit nor propriety existed. The figure was tall and
gaunt, and shrouded from head to foot in the habiliments of the grave. The mask
which concealed the visage was made so nearly to resemble the countenance of
a stiffened corpse that the closest scrutiny must have had difficulty in detecting
the cheat. And yet all this might have been endured, if not approved, by the mad
revellers around. But the mummer had gone so far as to assume the type of the
Red Death. His vesture was dabbled in *blood*—and his broad brow, with all the
features of the face, was besprinkled with the scarlet horror.

When the eyes of Prince Prospero fell upon this spectral image (which, with
a slow and solemn movement, as if more fully to sustain its *rôle*, stalked to and
fro among the waltzers) he was seen to be convulsed, in the first moment with a
strong shudder either of terror or distaste; but, in the next, his brow reddened
with rage.

"Who dares"—he demanded hoarsely of the courtiers who stood near him—
"who dares insult us with this blasphemous mockery? Seize him and unmask
him—that we may know whom we have to hang, at sunrise, from the battlements!"

It was in the eastern or blue chamber in which stood the Prince Prospero as
he uttered these words. They rang throughout the seven rooms loudly and

clearly, for the prince was a bold and robust man, and the music had become hushed at the waving of his hand.

It was in the blue room where stood the prince, with a group of pale courtiers by his side. At first, as he spoke, there was a slight rushing movement of this group in the direction of the intruder, who, at the moment was also near at hand, and now, with deliberate and stately step, made closer approach to the speaker. But from a certain nameless awe with which the mad assumptions of the mummer had inspired the whole party, there were found none who put forth hand to seize him; so that, unimpeded, he passed within a yard of the prince's person; and, while the vast assembly, as if with one impulse, shrank from the centres of the rooms to the walls, he made his way uninterruptedly, but with the same solemn and measured step which had distinguished him from the first, through the blue chamber to the purple—through the purple to the green—through the green to the orange—through this again to the white—and even thence to the violet, ere a decided movement had been made to arrest him. It was then, however, that the Prince Prospero, maddening with rage and the shame of his own momentary cowardice, rushed hurriedly through the six chambers, while none followed him on account of a deadly terror that had seized upon all. He bore aloft a drawn dagger, and had approached, in rapid impetuosity, to within three or four feet of the retreating figure, when the latter, having attained the extremity of the velvet apartment, turned suddenly and confronted his pursuer. There was a sharp cry— and the dagger dropped gleaming upon the sable carpet, upon which, instantly afterward, fell prostrate in death the Prince Prospero. Then, summoning the wild courage of despair, a throng of the revellers at once threw themselves into the black apartment, and, seizing the mummer, whose tall figure stood erect and motionless within the shadow of the ebony clock, gasped in unutterable horror at finding the grave cerements and corpse-like mask, which they handled with so violent a rudeness, untenanted by any tangible form.

And now was acknowledged the presence of the Red Death. He had come like a thief in the night. And one by one dropped the revellers in the blood-bedewed halls of their revel, and died each in the despairing posture of his fall. And the life of the ebony clock went out with that of the last of the gay. And the flames of the tripods expired. And Darkness and Decay and the Red Death held illimitable dominion over all.

The Tell-Tale Heart

TRUE!—nervous—very, very dreadfully nervous I had been and am; but why *will* you say that I am mad? The disease had sharpened my senses—not destroyed—not dulled them. Above all was the sense of hearing acute. I heard all things in the heaven and in the earth. I heard many things in hell. How, then, am I mad? Hearken! and observe how healthily—how calmly I can tell you the whole story.

It is impossible to say how first the idea entered my brain; but once conceived, it haunted me day and night. Object there was none. Passion there was none. I loved the old man. He had never wronged me. He had never given me insult. For his gold I had no desire. I think it was his eye! yes, it was this! One of his eyes resembled that of a vulture—a pale blue eye, with a film over it. Whenever it fell upon me, my blood ran cold; and so by degrees—very gradually—I made up my mind to take the life of the old man, and thus rid myself of the eye for ever.

Now this is the point. You fancy me mad. Madmen know nothing. But you should have seen *me*. You should have seen how wisely I proceeded—with what caution—with what foresight—with what dissimulation I went to work! I was never kinder to the old man than during the whole week before I killed him. And every night, about midnight, I turned the latch of his door and opened it— oh, so gently! And then, when I had made an opening sufficient for my head, I put in a dark lantern, all closed, closed, so that no light shone out, and then I thrust in my head. Oh, you would have laughed to see how cunningly I thrust it in! I moved it slowly—very, very slowly, so that I might not disturb the old man's sleep. It took me an hour to place my whole head within the opening so far that I could see him as he lay upon his bed. Ha!—would a madman have been so wise as this? And then, when my head was well in the room, I undid the lantern cautiously—oh, so cautiously—cautiously (for the hinges creaked)—I undid it just so much that a single thin ray fell upon the vulture eye. And this I did for seven long nights—every night just at midnight—but I found the eye always closed; and so it was impossible to do the work; for it was not the old man who vexed me, but his Evil Eye. And every morning, when the day broke, I went boldly into the chamber, and spoke courageously to him, calling him by name in a hearty tone, and inquiring how he had passed the night. So you see he would have been a very profound old man, indeed, to suspect that every night, just at twelve, I looked in upon him while he slept.

Upon the eighth night I was more than usually cautious in opening the door. A watch's minute hand moves more quickly than did mine. Never before that night had I *felt* the extent of my own powers—of my sagacity. I could scarcely contain my feelings of triumph. To think that there I was, opening the door, little by little, and he not even to dream of my secret deeds or thoughts. I fairly chuckled at the idea; and perhaps he heard me; for he moved on the bed suddenly, as if startled. Now you may think that I drew back—but no. His room was as black as pitch with the thick darkness (for the shutters were close fastened, through fear of robbers), and so I knew that he could not see the opening of the door, and I kept pushing it on steadily, steadily.

I had my head in, and was about to open the lantern, when my thumb slipped upon the tin fastening, and the old man sprang up in the bed, crying out—"Who's there?"

I kept quite still and said nothing. For a whole hour I did not move a muscle, and in the meantime I did not hear him lie down. He was still sitting up in the bed listening;—just as I have done, night after night, hearkening to the death watches in the wall.

Presently I heard a slight groan, and I knew it was the groan of mortal terror. It was not a groan of pain or of grief—oh, no!—it was the low stifled sound that arises from the bottom of the soul when overcharged with awe. I knew the sound well. Many a night, just at midnight, when all the world slept, it has welled up from my own bosom, deepening, with its dreadful echo, the terrors that distracted me. I say I knew it well. I knew what the old man felt, and pitied him, although I chuckled at heart. I knew that he had been lying awake ever since the first slight noise, when he had turned in the bed. His fears had been ever since growing upon him. He had been trying to fancy them causeless, but could not. He had been saying to himself—"It is nothing but the wind in the chimney—it is only a mouse crossing the floor," or "it is merely a cricket which has made a single chirp." Yes, he had been trying to comfort himself with these suppositions; but he had found all in vain. *All in vain*; because Death, in approaching him, had stalked with his black shadow before him, and enveloped the victim. And it was the mournful influence of the unperceived shadow that caused him to feel—although he neither saw nor heard—to *feel* the presence of my head within the room.

When I had waited a long time, very patiently, without hearing him lie down, I resolved to open a little—a very, very little crevice in the lantern. So

I opened it—you cannot imagine how stealthily, stealthily—until, at length, a single dim ray, like the thread of the spider, shot from out the crevice and full upon the vulture eye.

It was open—wide, wide open—and I grew furious as I gazed upon it. I saw it with perfect distinctness—all a dull blue, with a hideous veil over it that chilled the very marrow in my bones; but I could see nothing else of the old man's face or person: for I had directed the ray as if by instinct, precisely upon the damned spot.

And now have I not told you that what you mistake for madness is but over-acuteness of the senses?—now, I say, there came to my ears a low, dull, quick sound, such as a watch makes when enveloped in cotton. I knew *that* sound well too. It was the beating of the old man's heart. It increased my fury, as the beating of a drum stimulates the soldier into courage.

But even yet I refrained and kept still. I scarcely breathed. I held the lantern motionless. I tried how steadily I could maintain the ray upon the eye. Meantime the hellish tattoo of the heart increased. It grew quicker and quicker, and louder and louder every instant. The old man's terror *must* have been extreme! It grew louder, I say, louder every moment!—do you mark me well? I have told you that I am nervous: so I am. And now at the dead hour of the night, amid the dreadful silence of that old house, so strange a noise as this excited me to uncontrollable terror. Yet, for some minutes longer I refrained and stood still. But the beating grew louder, louder! I thought the heart must burst. And now a new anxiety seized me—the sound would be heard by a neighbor! The old man's hour had come! With a loud yell, I threw open the lantern and leaped into the room. He shrieked once—once only. In an instant I dragged him to the floor, and pulled the heavy bed over him. I then smiled gaily, to find the deed so far done. But, for many minutes, the heart beat on with a muffled sound. This, however, did not vex me; it would not be heard through the wall. At length it ceased. The old man was dead. I removed the bed and examined the corpse. Yes, he was stone, stone dead. I placed my hand upon the heart and held it there many minutes. There was no pulsation. He was stone dead. His eye would trouble me no more.

If still you think me mad, you will think so no longer when I describe the wise precautions I took for the concealment of the body. The night waned, and I worked hastily, but in silence. First of all I dismembered the corpse. I cut off the head and the arms and the legs.

I then took up three planks from the flooring of the chamber, and deposited all between the scantlings. I then replaced the boards so cleverly, so cunningly,

that no human eye—not even *his*—could have detected any thing wrong. There was nothing to wash out—no stain of any kind—no blood-spot whatever. I had been too wary for that. A tub had caught all—ha! ha!

When I had made an end of these labors, it was four o'clock—still dark as midnight. As the bell sounded the hour, there came a knocking at the street door. I went down to open it with a light heart,—for what had I *now* to fear? There entered three men, who introduced themselves, with perfect suavity, as officers of the police. A shriek had been heard by a neighbor during the night; suspicion of foul play had been aroused; information had been lodged at the police office, and they (the officers) had been deputed to search the premises.

I smiled,—for *what* had I to fear? I bade the gentlemen welcome. The shriek, I said, was my own in a dream. The old man, I mentioned, was absent in the country. I took my visitors all over the house. I bade them search—search *well*. I led them, at length, to *his* chamber. I showed them his treasures, secure, undisturbed. In the enthusiasm of my confidence, I brought chairs into the room, and desired them *here* to rest from their fatigues, while I myself, in the wild audacity of my perfect triumph, placed my own seat upon the very spot beneath which reposed the corpse of the victim.

The officers were satisfied. My *manner* had convinced them. I was singularly at ease. They sat, and while I answered cheerily, they chatted familiar things. But, ere long, I felt myself getting pale and wished them gone. My head ached, and I fancied a ringing in my ears; but still they sat and still chatted. The ringing became more distinct:—it continued and became more distinct: I talked more freely to get rid of the feeling; but it continued and gained definitiveness—until, at length, I found that the noise was *not* within my ears.

No doubt I now grew *very* pale;—but I talked more fluently, and with a heightened voice. Yet the sound increased—and what could I do? It was *a low, dull, quick sound—much such a sound as a watch makes when enveloped in cotton.* I gasped for breath—and yet the officers heard it not. I talked more quickly—more vehemently; but the noise steadily increased. I arose and argued about trifles, in a high key and with violent gesticulations, but the noise steadily increased. Why *would* they not be gone? I paced the floor to and fro with heavy strides, as if excited to fury by the observation of the men—but the noise steadily increased. Oh God! what *could* I do? I foamed—I raved—I swore! I swung the chair upon which I had been sitting, and grated it upon the boards, but the noise arose over all and continually increased. It grew louder—louder—*louder!* And still the men chatted pleasantly, and smiled. Was it possible they heard not? Almighty

God!—no, no! They heard!—they suspected!—they *knew!*—they were making a mockery of my horror!—this I thought, and this I think. But any thing was better than this agony! Any thing was more tolerable than this derision! I could bear those hypocritical smiles no longer! I felt that I must scream or die!—and now—again!—hark! louder! louder! louder! *louder!*—

"Villains!" I shrieked, "dissemble no more! I admit the deed!—tear up the planks!—here, here!—it is the beating of his hideous heart!"

The Fall of the House of Usher

Son cœur est un luth suspendu;
Sitôt qu'on le touche il résonne.
— DE BÉRANGER

URING the whole of a dull, dark, and soundless day in the autumn of the year, when the clouds hung oppressively low in the heavens, I had been passing alone, on horseback, through a singularly dreary tract of country, and at length found myself, as the shades of the evening drew on, within view of the melancholy House of Usher. I know not how it was—but, with the first glimpse of the building, a sense of insufferable gloom pervaded my spirit. I say insufferable; for the feeling was unrelieved by any of that half-pleasurable, because poetic, sentiment with which the mind usually receives even the sternest natural images of the desolate or terrible. I looked upon the scene before me—

upon the mere house, and the simple landscape features of the domain—upon the bleak walls—upon the vacant eye-like windows—upon a few rank sedges—and upon a few white trunks of decayed trees—with an utter depression of soul which I can compare to no earthly sensation more properly than to the after-dream of the reveller upon opium—the bitter lapse into every-day life—the hideous dropping off of the veil. There was an iciness, a sinking, a sickening of the heart—an unredeemed dreariness of thought which no goading of the imagination could torture into aught of the sublime. What was it—I paused to think—what was it that so unnerved me in the contemplation of the House of Usher? It was a mystery all insoluble; nor could I grapple with the shadowy fancies that crowded upon me as I pondered. I was forced to fall back upon the unsatisfactory conclusion, that while, beyond doubt, there *are* combinations of very simple natural objects which have the power of thus affecting us, still the analysis of this power lies among considerations beyond our depth. It was possible, I reflected, that a mere different arrangement of the particulars of the scene, of the details of the picture, would be sufficient to modify, or perhaps to annihilate its capacity for sorrowful impression; and, acting upon this idea, I reined my horse to the precipitous brink of a black and lurid tarn that lay in unruffled lustre by the dwelling, and gazed down—but with a shudder even more thrilling than before—upon the remodelled and inverted images of the gray sedge, and the ghastly tree-stems, and the vacant and eye-like windows.

Nevertheless, in this mansion of gloom I now proposed to myself a sojourn of some weeks. Its proprietor, Roderick Usher, had been one of my boon companions in boyhood; but many years had elapsed since our last meeting. A letter, however, had lately reached me in a distant part of the country—a letter from him—which, in its wildly importunate nature, had admitted of no other than a personal reply. The MS. gave evidence of nervous agitation. The writer spoke of acute bodily illness—of a mental disorder which oppressed him—and of an earnest desire to see me, as his best and indeed his only personal friend, with a view of attempting, by the cheerfulness of my society, some alleviation of his malady. It was the manner in which all this, and much more, was said—it was the apparent *heart* that went with his request—which allowed me no room for hesitation; and I accordingly obeyed forthwith what I still considered a very singular summons.

Although, as boys, we had been even intimate associates, yet I really knew little of my friend. His reserve had been always excessive and habitual. I was aware, however, that his very ancient family had been noted, time out of mind, for a peculiar sensibility of temperament, displaying itself, through long ages, in many

works of exalted art, and manifested, of late, in repeated deeds of munificent yet unobtrusive charity, as well as in a passionate devotion to the intricacies, perhaps even more than to the orthodox and easily recognizable beauties, of musical science. I had learned, too, the very remarkable fact, that the stem of the Usher race, all time-honored as it was, had put forth, at no period, any enduring branch; in other words, that the entire family lay in the direct line of descent, and had always, with very trifling and very temporary variation, so lain. It was this deficiency, I considered, while running over in thought the perfect keeping of the character of the premises with the accredited character of the people, and while speculating upon the possible influence which the one, in the long lapse of centuries, might have exercised upon the other—it was this deficiency, perhaps, of collateral issue, and the consequent undeviating transmission, from sire to son, of the patrimony with the name, which had, at length, so identified the two as to merge the original title of the estate in the quaint and equivocal appellation of the "House of Usher"—an appellation which seemed to include, in the minds of the peasantry who used it, both the family and the family mansion.

I have said that the sole effect of my somewhat childish experiment—that of looking down within the tarn—had been to deepen the first singular impression. There can be no doubt that the consciousness of the rapid increase of my superstition—for why should I not so term it?—served mainly to accelerate the increase itself. Such, I have long known, is the paradoxical law of all sentiments having terror as a basis. And it might have been for this reason only, that, when I again uplifted my eyes to the house itself, from its image in the pool, there grew in my mind a strange fancy—a fancy so ridiculous, indeed, that I but mention it to show the vivid force of the sensations which oppressed me. I had so worked upon my imagination as really to believe that about the whole mansion and domain there hung an atmosphere peculiar to themselves and their immediate vicinity—an atmosphere which had no affinity with the air of heaven, but which had reeked up from the decayed trees, and the gray wall, and the silent tarn—a pestilent and mystic vapor, dull, sluggish, faintly discernible, and leaden-hued.

Shaking off from my spirit what *must* have been a dream, I scanned more narrowly the real aspect of the building. Its principal feature seemed to be that of an excessive antiquity. The discoloration of ages had been great. Minute fungi overspread the whole exterior, hanging in a fine tangled web-work from the eaves. Yet all this was apart from any extraordinary dilapidation. No portion of the masonry had fallen; and there appeared to be a wild inconsistency between its still perfect adaptation of parts, and the crumbling condition of the individual stones. In this there was much that reminded me of the specious totality of old wood-work which has rotted for long years in some neglected vault, with no disturbance from the breath of the external air. Beyond this indication of extensive decay, however, the fabric gave little token of instability. Perhaps the eye of a scrutinizing observer might have discovered a barely perceptible fissure, which, extending from the roof of the building in front, made its way down the wall in a zigzag direction, until it became lost in the sullen waters of the tarn.

Noticing these things, I rode over a short causeway to the house. A servant in waiting took my horse, and I entered the Gothic archway of the hall. A valet, of stealthy step, thence conducted me, in silence, through many dark and intricate passages in my progress to the *studio* of his master. Much that I encountered on the way contributed, I know not how, to heighten the vague sentiments of which I have already spoken. While the objects around me—while the carvings of the ceilings, the sombre tapestries of the walls, the ebon blackness of the floors, and the phantasmagoric armorial trophies which rattled as I strode, were but matters to which, or to such as which, I had been accustomed from my infancy—while I hesitated not to acknowledge how familiar was all this—I still wondered to find how unfamiliar were the fancies which ordinary images were stirring up. On one of the staircases, I met the physician of the family. His countenance, I thought, wore a mingled expression of low cunning and perplexity. He accosted me with trepidation and passed on. The valet now threw open a door and ushered me into the presence of his master.

The room in which I found myself was very large and lofty. The windows were long, narrow, and pointed, and at so vast a distance from the black oaken floor as to be altogether inaccessible from within. Feeble gleams of encrimsoned light made their way through the trellissed panes, and served to render sufficiently distinct the more prominent objects around; the eye, however, struggled in vain to reach the remoter angles of the chamber, or the recesses of the vaulted and fretted ceiling. Dark draperies hung upon the walls. The general furniture was profuse, comfortless, antique, and tattered. Many books and musical instruments lay scattered about, but failed to give any vitality to the scene. I felt that I breathed an atmosphere of sorrow. An air of stern, deep, and irredeemable gloom hung over and pervaded all.

Upon my entrance, Usher arose from a sofa on which he had been lying at full length, and greeted me with a vivacious warmth which had much in it, I at first thought, of an overdone cordiality—of the constrained effort of the *ennuyé* man of the world. A glance, however, at his countenance convinced me of his perfect sincerity. We sat down; and for some moments, while he spoke not, I gazed upon him with a feeling half of pity, half of awe. Surely, man had never

before so terribly altered, in so brief a period, as had Roderick Usher! It was with difficulty that I could bring myself to admit the identity of the wan being before me with the companion of my early boyhood. Yet the character of his face had been at all times remarkable. A cadaverousness of complexion; an eye large, liquid, and luminous beyond comparison; lips somewhat thin and very pallid, but of a surpassingly beautiful curve; a nose of a delicate Hebrew model, but with a breadth of nostril unusual in similar formations; a finely moulded chin, speaking, in its want of prominence, of a want of moral energy; hair of a more than web-like softness and tenuity;—these features, with an inordinate expansion above the regions of the temple, made up altogether a countenance not easily to be forgotten. And now in the mere exaggeration of the prevailing character of these features, and of the expression they were wont to convey, lay so much of change that I doubted to whom I spoke. The now ghastly pallor of the skin, and the now miraculous lustre of the eye, above all things startled and even awed me. The silken hair, too, had been suffered to grow all unheeded, and as, in its wild gossamer texture, it floated rather than fell about the face, I could not, even with effort, connect its Arabesque expression with any idea of simple humanity.

In the manner of my friend I was at once struck with an incoherence—an inconsistency; and I soon found this to arise from a series of feeble and futile struggles to overcome an habitual trepidancy—an excessive nervous agitation. For something of this nature I had indeed been prepared, no less by his letter, than by reminiscences of certain boyish traits, and by conclusions deduced from his peculiar physical confirmation and temperament. His action was alternately vivacious and sullen. His voice varied rapidly from a tremulous indecision (when the animal spirits seemed utterly in abeyance) to that species of energetic concision—that abrupt, weighty, unhurried, and hollow-sounding enunciation—that leaden, self-balanced, and perfectly modulated guttural utterance, which may be observed in the lost drunkard, or the irreclaimable eater of opium, during the periods of his most intense excitement.

It was thus that he spoke of the object of my visit, of his earnest desire to see me, and of the solace he expected me to afford him. He entered, at some length, into what he conceived to be the nature of his malady. It was, he said, a constitutional and a family evil, and one for which he despaired to find a remedy—a mere nervous affection, he immediately added, which would undoubtedly soon pass off. It displayed itself in a host of unnatural sensations. Some of these, as he detailed them, interested and bewildered me; although, perhaps, the terms and the general manner of their narration had their weight. He suffered much from a morbid acuteness of the senses; the most insipid food was alone endurable;

he could wear only garments of certain texture; the odors of all flowers were oppressive; his eyes were tortured by even a faint light; and there were but peculiar sounds, and these from stringed instruments, which did not inspire him with horror.

To an anomalous species of terror I found him a bounden slave. "I shall perish," said he, "I *must* perish in this deplorable folly. Thus, thus, and not otherwise, shall I be lost. I dread the events of the future, not in themselves, but in their results. I shudder at the thought of any, even the most trivial, incident, which may operate upon this intolerable agitation of soul. I have, indeed, no abhorrence of danger, except in its absolute effect—in terror. In this unnerved, in this pitiable, condition I feel that the period will sooner or later arrive when I must abandon life and reason together, in some struggle with the grim phantasm, FEAR."

I learned, moreover, at intervals, and through broken and equivocal hints, another singular feature of his mental condition. He was enchained by certain superstitious impressions in regard to the dwelling which he tenanted, and whence, for many years, he had never ventured forth—in regard to an influence whose supposititious force was conveyed in terms too shadowy here to be re-stated—an influence which some peculiarities in the mere form and substance of his family mansion had, by dint of long sufferance, he said, obtained over his spirit—an effect which the *physique* of the gray walls and turrets, and of the dim tarn into which they all looked down, had, at length, brought about upon the *morale* of his existence.

He admitted, however, although with hesitation, that much of the peculiar gloom which thus afflicted him could be traced to a more natural and far more palpable origin—to the severe and long-continued illness—indeed to the evidently approaching dissolution—of a tenderly beloved sister, his sole companion for long years, his last and only relative on earth. "Her decease," he said, with a bitterness which I can never forget, "would leave him (him, the hopeless and the frail) the last of the ancient race of the Ushers." While he spoke, the lady Madeline (for so was she called) passed through a remote portion of the apartment, and, without having noticed my presence, disappeared. I regarded her with an utter astonishment not unmingled with dread; and yet I found it impossible to account for such feelings. A sensation of stupor oppressed me as my eyes followed her retreating steps. When a door, at length, closed upon her, my glance sought instinctively and eagerly the countenance of the brother; but he had buried his face in his hands, and I could only perceive that a far more than ordinary wanness had overspread the emaciated fingers through which trickled many passionate tears.

The disease of the lady Madeline had long baffled the skill of her physicians. A settled apathy, a gradual wasting away of the person, and frequent although transient affections of a partially cataleptical character were the unusual diagnosis. Hitherto she had steadily borne up against the pressure of her malady, and had not betaken herself finally to bed; but on the closing in of the evening of my arrival at the house, she succumbed (as her brother told me at night with inexpressible agitation) to the prostrating power of the destroyer; and I learned that the glimpse I had obtained of her person would thus probably be the last I should obtain—that the lady, at least while living, would be seen by me no more.

For several days ensuing, her name was unmentioned by either Usher or myself; and during this period I was busied in earnest endeavors to alleviate the melancholy of my friend. We painted and read together, or I listened, as if in a dream, to the wild improvisations of his speaking guitar. And thus, as a closer and still closer intimacy admitted me more unreservedly into the recesses of his spirit, the more bitterly did I perceive the futility of all attempt at cheering a mind from which darkness, as if an inherent positive quality, poured forth upon all objects of the moral and physical universe in one unceasing radiation of gloom.

I shall ever bear about me a memory of the many solemn hours I thus spent alone with the master of the House of Usher. Yet I should fail in any attempt to convey an idea of the exact character of the studies, or of the occupations, in which he involved me, or led me the way. An excited and highly distempered ideality threw a sulphureous lustre over all. His long improvised dirges will ring forever in my ears. Among other things, I hold painfully in mind a certain singular perversion and amplification of the wild air of the last waltz of Von Weber. From the paintings over which his elaborate fancy brooded, and which grew, touch by touch, into vaguenesses at which I shuddered the more thrillingly, because I shuddered knowing not why—from these paintings (vivid as their images now are before me) I would in vain endeavor to educe more than a small portion which should lie within the compass of merely written words. By the utter simplicity, by the nakedness of his designs, he arrested and overawed attention. If ever mortal painted an idea, that mortal was Roderick Usher. For me at least, in the circumstances then surrounding me, there arose out of the pure abstractions which the hypochondriac contrived to throw upon his canvas, an intensity of intolerable awe, no shadow of which felt I ever yet in the contemplation of the certainly glowing yet too concrete reveries of Fuseli.

One of the phantasmagoric conceptions of my friend, partaking not so rigidly of the spirit of abstraction, may be shadowed forth, although feebly, in words. A small picture presented the interior of an immensely long and rectangular vault or tunnel, with low walls, smooth, white, and without interruption or device. Certain accessory points of the design served well to convey the idea that this excavation lay at an exceeding depth below the surface of the earth. No outlet was observed in any portion of its vast extent, and no torch or other artificial source of light was discernible; yet a flood of intense rays rolled throughout, and bathed the whole in a ghastly and inappropriate splendor.

I have just spoken of that morbid condition of the auditory nerve which rendered all music intolerable to the sufferer, with the exception of certain effects of stringed instruments. It was, perhaps, the narrow limits to which he thus confined himself upon the guitar which gave birth, in great measure, to the fantastic character of his performances. But the fervid *facility* of his *impromptus* could not be so accounted for. They must have been, and were, in the notes, as well as in the words of his wild fantasias (for he not unfrequently accompanied himself with rhymed verbal improvisations), the result of that intense mental collectedness and concentration to which I have previously alluded as observable only in particular moments of the highest artificial excitement. The words of one of these rhapsodies I have easily remembered. I was, perhaps, the more forcibly impressed with it as he gave it, because, in the under or mystic current of its meaning, I fancied that I perceived, and for the first time, a full consciousness on the part of Usher of the tottering of his lofty reason upon her throne. The verses, which were entitled "The Haunted Palace," ran very nearly, if not accurately, thus:—

I.

In the greenest of our valleys,
        By good angels tenanted,
Once a fair and stately palace—
        Radiant palace—reared its head.
In the monarch Thought's dominion—
        It stood there!
Never seraph spread a pinion
        Over fabric half so fair.

II.

Banners yellow, glorious, golden,
        On its roof did float and flow
(This—all this—was in the olden
        Time long ago);
And every gentle air that dallied,
        In that sweet day,
Along the ramparts plumed and pallid,
        A winged odor went away.

III.

Wanderers in that happy valley
  Through two luminous windows saw
Spirits moving musically
  To a lute's well-tunéd law;
Round about a throne, where sitting
  (Porphyrogene!)
In state his glory well befitting,
  The ruler of the realm was seen.

IV.

And all with pearl and ruby glowing
  Was the fair palace door,
Through which came flowing, flowing, flowing
  And sparkling evermore,
A troop of Echoes whose sweet duty
  Was but to sing,
In voices of surpassing beauty,
  The wit and wisdom of their king.

V.

But evil things, in robes of sorrow,
  Assailed the monarch's high estate;
(Ah, let us mourn, for never morrow
  Shall dawn upon him, desolate!)
And, round about his home, the glory
  That blushed and bloomed

Is but a dim-remembered story
Of the old time entombed.

VI.

And travellers now within that valley.
Through the red-litten windows see
Vast forms that move fantastically
To a discordant melody;
While, like a rapid ghastly river,
Through the pale door,
A hideous throng rush out forever,
And laugh—but smile no more.

I well remember that suggestions arising from this ballad led us into a train of thought wherein there became manifest an opinion of Usher's, which I mention not so much on account of its novelty (for other men have thought thus), as on account of the pertinacity with which he maintained it. This opinion, in its general form, was that of the sentience of all vegetable things. But, in his disordered fancy, the idea had assumed a more daring character, and trespassed, under certain conditions, upon the kingdom of inorganization. I lack words to express the full extent, or the earnest *abandon* of his persuasion. The belief, however, was connected (as I have previously hinted) with the gray stones of the home of his forefathers. The conditions of the sentience had been here, he imagined, fulfilled in the method of collocation of these stones—in the order of their arrangement, as well as in that of the many *fungi* which overspread them, and of the decayed trees which stood around—above all, in the long undisturbed endurance of this arrangement, and in its reduplication in the still waters of the tarn. Its evidence—the evidence of the sentience—was to be seen, he said (and I here started as he spoke), in the gradual yet certain condensation of an atmosphere of their own about the waters and the walls. The result was discoverable, he added, in that silent yet importunate and terrible influence which for centuries had moulded the destinies of his family, and which made *him* what I now saw him— what he was. Such opinions need no comment, and I will make none.

Our books—the books which, for years, had formed no small portion of the mental existence of the invalid—were, as might be supposed, in strict keeping with this character of phantasm. We pored together over such works as the "Ververt et Chartreuse" of Gresset; the "Belphegor" of Machiavelli; the "Heaven and Hell" of Swedenborg; the "Subterranean Voyage of Nicholas Klimm" by Holberg; the "Chiromancy" of Robert Flud, of Jean D'Indaginé, and of Dela Chambre; the "Journey into the Blue Distance of Tieck"; and the "City of the Sun of Campanella." One favorite volume was a small octavo edition of the

"Directorium Inquisitorium," by the Dominican Eymeric de Gironne; and there were passages in Pomponius Mela, about the old African Satyrs and Œgipans, over which Usher would sit dreaming for hours. His chief delight, however, was found in the perusal of an exceedingly rare and curious book in quarto Gothic—the manual of a forgotten church—the *Vigiliæ Mortuorum secundum Chorum Ecclesiæ Maguntinæ.*

I could not help thinking of the wild ritual of this work, and of its probable influence upon the hypochondriac, when, one evening, having informed me abruptly that the lady Madeline was no more, he stated his intention of preserving her corpse for a fortnight (previously to its final interment), in one of the numerous vaults within the main walls of the building. The worldly reason, however, assigned for this singular proceeding, was one which I did not feel at liberty to dispute. The brother had been led to his resolution (so he told me) by consideration of the unusual character of the malady of the deceased, of certain obtrusive and eager inquiries on the part of her medical men, and of the remote and exposed situation of the burial-ground of the family. I will not deny that when I called to mind the sinister countenance of the person whom I met upon the staircase, on the day of my arrival at the house, I had no desire to oppose what I regarded as at best but a harmless, and by no means an unnatural, precaution.

At the request of Usher, I personally aided him in the arrangements for the temporary entombment. The body having been encoffined, we two alone bore it to its rest. The vault in which we placed it (and which had been so long unopened that our torches, half smothered in its oppressive atmosphere, gave us little opportunity for investigation) was small, damp, and entirely without means of admission for light; lying, at great depth, immediately beneath that portion of the building in which was my own sleeping apartment. It had been used, apparently, in remote feudal times, for the worst purposes of a donjon-keep, and, in later days, as a place of deposit for powder, or some other highly combustible substance, as a portion of its floor, and the whole interior of a long archway through which we reached it, were carefully sheathed with copper. The door, of massive iron, had been, also, similarly protected. Its immense weight caused an unusually sharp, grating sound, as it moved upon its hinges.

Having deposited our mournful burden upon tressels within this region of horror, we partially turned aside the yet unscrewed lid of the coffin, and looked upon the face of the tenant. A striking similitude between the brother and sister now first arrested my attention; and Usher, divining, perhaps, my thoughts, murmured out some few words from which I learned that the deceased and himself had been twins, and that sympathies of a scarcely intelligible nature had always existed between them. Our glances, however, rested not long upon the dead—for we could not regard her unawed. The disease which had thus entombed the lady in the maturity of youth, had left, as usual in all maladies of a strictly cataleptical character, the mockery of a faint blush upon the bosom and the face, and that suspiciously lingering smile upon the lip which is so terrible in death. We replaced and screwed down the lid, and, having secured the door of iron, made our way, with toil, into the scarcely less gloomy apartments of the upper portion of the house.

And now, some days of bitter grief having elapsed, an observable change came over the features of the mental disorder of my friend. His ordinary manner had vanished. His ordinary occupations were neglected or forgotten. He roamed from chamber to chamber with hurried, unequal, and objectless step. The pallor of his countenance had assumed, if possible, a more ghastly hue—but the luminousness of his eye had utterly gone out. The once occasional huskiness of his tone was heard no more; and a tremulous quaver, as if of extreme terror, habitually characterized his utterance. There were times, indeed, when I thought his unceasingly agitated mind was laboring with some oppressive secret, to divulge which he struggled for the necessary courage. At times, again, I was obliged to resolve all into the mere inexplicable vagaries of madness, for I beheld

him gazing upon vacancy for long hours, in an attitude of the profoundest attention, as if listening to some imaginary sound. It was no wonder that his condition terrified—that it infected me. I felt creeping upon me, by slow yet certain
degrees, the wild influences of his own fantastic yet impressive superstitions.

It was, especially, upon retiring to bed late in the night of the seventh or
eighth day after the placing of the lady Madeline within the donjon, that I experienced the full power of such feelings. Sleep came not near my couch—while the
hours waned and waned away. I struggled to reason off the nervousness which
had dominion over me. I endeavored to believe that much, if not all of what I
felt, was due to the bewildering influence of the gloomy furniture of the room—
of the dark and tattered draperies, which, tortured into motion by the breath of
a rising tempest, swayed fitfully to and fro upon the walls, and rustled uneasily
about the decorations of the bed. But my efforts were fruitless. An irrepressible
tremor gradually pervaded my frame; and, at length, there sat upon my very heart
an incubus of utterly causeless alarm. Shaking this off with a gasp and a struggle,
I uplifted myself upon the pillows, and, peering earnestly within the intense
darkness of the chamber, hearkened—I know not why, except that an instinctive
spirit prompted me—to certain low and indefinite sounds which came, through
the pauses of the storm, at long intervals, I knew not whence. Overpowered by

an intense sentiment of horror, unaccountable yet unendurable, I threw on my clothes with haste (for I felt that I should sleep no more during the night), and endeavored to arouse myself from the pitiable condition into which I had fallen, by pacing rapidly to and fro through the apartment.

I had taken but few turns in this manner, when a light step on an adjoining staircase arrested my attention. I presently recognized it as that of Usher. In an instant afterward he rapped, with a gentle touch, at my door, and entered, bearing a lamp. His countenance was, as usual, cadaverously wan—but, moreover, there was a species of mad hilarity in his eyes—an evidently restrained *hysteria* in his whole demeanor. His air appalled me—but anything was preferable to the solitude which I had so long endured, and I even welcomed his presence as a relief.

"And you have not seen it?" he said abruptly, after having stared about him for some moments in silence—"you have not then seen it?—but, stay! you shall." Thus speaking, and having carefully shaded his lamp, he hurried to one of the casements, and threw it freely open to the storm.

The impetuous fury of the entering gust nearly lifted us from our feet. It was, indeed, a tempestuous yet sternly beautiful night, and one wildly singular in its terror and its beauty. A whirlwind had apparently collected its force in our vicinity; for there were frequent and violent alterations in the direction of the wind; and the exceeding density of the clouds (which hung so low as to press upon the turrets of the house) did not prevent our perceiving the life-like velocity with which they flew careering from all points against each other, without passing away into the distance. I say that even their exceeding density did not prevent our perceiving this—yet we had no glimpse of the moon or stars, nor was there any flashing forth of the lightning. But the under surfaces of the huge masses of agitated vapor, as well as all terrestrial objects immediately around us, were glowing in the unnatural light of a faintly luminous and distinctly visible gaseous exhalation which hung about and enshrouded the mansion.

"You must not—you shall not behold this!" said I, shuddering, to Usher, as I led him, with a gentle violence, from the window to a seat. "These appearances, which bewilder you, are merely electrical phenomena not uncommon—or it may be that they have their ghastly origin in the rank miasma of the tarn. Let us close this casement;—the air is chilling and dangerous to your frame. Here is one of your favorite romances. I will read, and you shall listen:—and so we will pass away this terrible night together."

The antique volume which I had taken up was the "Mad Trist" of Sir Launcelot Canning; but I had called it a favorite of Usher's more in sad jest than in earnest; for, in truth, there is little in its uncouth and unimaginative prolixity which could have had interest for the lofty and spiritual ideality of my friend. It was, however, the only book immediately at hand; and I indulged a vague hope that the excitement which now agitated the hypochondriac, might find relief (for the history of mental disorder is full of similar anomalies) even in the extremeness of the folly which I should read. Could I have judged, indeed, by the wild overstrained air of vivacity with which he hearkened, or apparently hearkened, to the words of the tale, I might well have congratulated myself upon the success of my design.

I had arrived at that well-known portion of the story where Ethelred, the hero of the Trist, having sought in vain for peaceable admission into the dwelling of the hermit, proceeds to make good an entrance by force. Here, it will be remembered, the words of the narrative run thus:

"And Ethelred, who was by nature of a doughty heart, and who was now mighty withal, on account of the powerfulness of the wine which he had drunken, waited no longer to hold parley with the hermit, who, in sooth, was of an obstinate and maliceful turn, but, feeling the rain upon his shoulders, and fearing the rising of the tempest, uplifted his mace outright, and, with blows, made quickly room in the plankings of the door for his gauntleted hand; and now pulling therewith sturdily, he so cracked, and ripped, and tore all asunder, that the noise of the dry and hollow-sounding wood alarumed and reverberated throughout the forest."

At the termination of this sentence I started and, for a moment, paused; for it appeared to me (although I at once concluded that my excited fancy had deceived me)—it appeared to me that, from some very remote portion of the mansion, there came, indistinctly to my ears, what might have been, in its exact similarity of character, the echo (but a stifled and dull one certainly) of the very cracking and ripping sound which Sir Launcelot had so particularly described. It was, beyond doubt, the coincidence alone which had arrested my attention; for, amid the rattling of the sashes of the casements, and the ordinary commingled noises of the still increasing storm, the sound, in itself, had nothing, surely, which should have interested or disturbed me. I continued the story:

"But the good champion Ethelred, now entering within the door, was sore enraged and amazed to perceive no signal of the maliceful hermit; but, in the stead thereof, a dragon of a scaly and prodigious demeanor, and of a fiery tongue, which sate in guard before a palace of gold, with a floor of silver; and upon the wall there hung a shield of shining brass with this legend enwritten—

Who entereth herein, a conqueror hath bin;
Who slayeth the dragon, the shield he shall win.

And Ethelred uplifted his mace, and struck upon the head of the dragon, which fell before him, and gave up his pesty breath, with a shriek so horrid and harsh, and withal so piercing, that Ethelred had fain to close his ears with his hands against the dreadful noise of it, the like whereof was never before heard."

Here again I paused abruptly, and now with a feeling of wild amazement—for there could be no doubt whatever that, in this instance, I did actually hear (although from what direction it proceeded I found it impossible to say) a low and apparently distant, but harsh, protracted, and most unusual screaming or grating sound—the exact counterpart of what my fancy had already conjured up for the dragon's unnatural shriek as described by the romancer.

Oppressed, as I certainly was, upon the occurrence of this second and most extraordinary coincidence, by a thousand conflicting sensations, in which wonder and extreme terror were predominant, I still retained sufficient presence of mind to avoid exciting, by any observation, the sensitive nervousness of my companion. I was by no means certain that he had noticed the sounds in question; although, assuredly, a strange alteration had, during the last few minutes, taken place in his demeanor. From a position fronting my own, he had gradually brought round his chair, so as to sit with his face to the door of the chamber; and thus I could but partially perceive his features, although I saw that his lips trembled as if he were murmuring inaudibly. His head had dropped upon his breast—yet I knew that he was not asleep, from the wide and rigid opening of the eye as I caught a glance of it in profile. The motion of his body, too, was at variance with this idea—for he rocked from side to side with a gentle yet constant and uniform sway. Having rapidly taken notice of all this, I resumed the narrative of Sir Launcelot, which thus proceeded:

"And now, the champion, having escaped from the terrible fury of the dragon, bethinking himself of the brazen shield, and of the breaking up of the enchantment which was upon it, removed the carcass from out of the way before him, and approached valorously over the silver pavement of the castle to where the shield was upon the wall; which in sooth tarried not for his full coming, but fell down at his feet upon the silver floor, with a mighty great and terrible ringing sound."

No sooner had these syllables passed my lips, than—as if a shield of brass had indeed, at the moment, fallen heavily upon a floor of silver—I became aware of a distinct, hollow, metallic, and clangorous, yet apparently muffled, reverberation.

Completely unnerved, I leaped to my feet; but the measured rocking movement of Usher was undisturbed. I rushed to the chair in which he sat. His eyes were bent fixedly before him, and throughout his whole countenance there reigned a stony rigidity. But, as I placed my hand upon his shoulder, there came a strong shudder over his whole person; a sickly smile quivered about his lips; and I saw that he spoke in a low, hurried, and gibbering murmur, as if unconscious of my presence. Bending closely over him, I at length drank in the hideous import of his words.

"Not hear it?—yes, I hear it, and *have* heard it. Long—long—long—many minutes, many hours, many days, have I heard it—yet I dared not—oh, pity me, miserable wretch that I am!—I dared not—I *dared* not speak! *We have put her living in the tomb!* Said I not that my senses were acute? I *now* tell you that I heard her first feeble movements in the hollow coffin. I heard them—many, many days ago—yet I dared not—*I dared not speak!* And now—to-night—Ethelred—ha! ha!— the breaking of the hermit's door, and the death-cry of the dragon, and the clangor of the shield—say, rather, the rending of her coffin, and the grating of the iron hinges of her prison, and her struggles within the coppered archway of the vault! Oh! whither shall I fly? Will she not be here anon? Is she not hurrying to upbraid me for my haste? Have I not heard her footstep on the stair? Do I not

distinguish that heavy and horrible beating of her heart? Madman!"—here he sprang furiously to his feet, and shrieked out his syllables, as if in the effort he were giving up his soul—*"Madman! I tell you that she now stands without the door!"*

As if in the superhuman energy of his utterance there had been found the potency of a spell, the huge antique panels to which the speaker pointed threw slowly back, upon the instant, their ponderous and ebony jaws. It was the work of the rushing gust—but then without those doors there *did* stand the lofty and enshrouded figure of the lady Madeline of Usher. There was blood upon her white robes, and the evidence of some bitter struggle upon every portion of her emaciated frame. For a moment she remained trembling and reeling to and fro upon the threshold—then, with a low moaning cry, fell heavily inward upon the person of her brother, and in her violent and now final death-agonies, bore him to the floor a corpse, and a victim to the terrors he had anticipated.

From that chamber, and from that mansion, I fled aghast. The storm was still abroad in all its wrath as I found myself crossing the old causeway. Suddenly there shot along the path a wild light, and I turned to see whence a gleam so unusual could have issued; for the vast house and its shadows were alone behind me. The radiance was that of the full, setting, and blood-red moon, which now shone vividly through that once barely discernible fissure, of which I have before spoken as extending from the roof of the building, in a zigzag direction, to the base. While I gazed, this fissure rapidly widened—there came a fierce breath of the whirlwind—the entire orb of the satellite burst at once upon my sight—my brain reeled as I saw the mighty walls rushing asunder—there was a long tumultuous shouting sound like the voice of a thousand waters—and the deep and dank tarn at my feet closed sullenly and silently over the fragments of the "*House of Usher.*"

The Murders in the Rue Morgue

*What song the Syrens sang, or what name Achilles assumed when he hid
himself among women, although puzzling questions, are not beyond
all conjecture.*

—S IR T HOMAS B ROWNE

T HE mental features discoursed of as the analytical, are, in themselves,
but little susceptible of analysis. We appreciate them only in their
effects. We know of them, among other things, that they are always to
their possessor, when inordinately possessed, a source of the liveliest enjoyment.
As the strong man exults in his physical ability, delighting in such exercises as call
his muscles into action, so glories the analyst in that moral activity which *disen-
tangles*. He derives pleasure from even the most trivial occupations bringing his
talent into play. He is fond of enigmas, of conundrums, hieroglyphics; exhibiting
in his solutions of each a degree of *acumen* which appears to the ordinary appre-

hension præternatural. His results, brought about by the very soul and essence of method, have, in truth, the whole air of intuition.

The faculty of re-solution is possibly much invigorated by mathematical study, and especially by that highest branch of it which, unjustly, and merely on account of its retrograde operations, has been called, as if *par excellence*, analysis. Yet to calculate is not in itself to analyse. A chess-player, for example, does the one, without effort at the other. It follows that the game of chess, in its effects upon mental character, is greatly misunderstood. I am not now writing a treatise, but simply prefacing a somewhat peculiar narrative by observations very much at random; I will, therefore, take occasion to assert that the higher powers of the reflective intellect are more decidedly and more usefully tasked by the unostentatious game of draughts than by all the elaborate frivolity of chess. In this latter, where the pieces have different and *bizarre* motions, with various and variable values, what is only complex, is mistaken (a not unusual error) for what is profound. The *attention* is here called powerfully into play. If it flag for an instant, an oversight is committed, resulting in injury or defeat. The possible moves being not only manifold, but involute, the chances of such oversights are multiplied; and in nine cases out of ten, it is the more concentrative rather than the more acute player who conquers. In draughts, on the contrary, where the moves are *unique* and have but little variation, the probabilities of inadvertence are diminished, and the mere attention being left comparatively unemployed, what advantages are obtained by either party are obtained by superior *acumen*. To be less abstract, let us suppose a game of draughts where the pieces are reduced to four kings, and where, of course, no oversight is to be expected. It is obvious that here the victory can be decided (the players being at all equal) only by some *recherché* movement, the result of some strong exertion of the intellect. Deprived of ordinary resources, the analyst throws himself into the spirit of his opponent, identifies himself therewith, and not unfrequently sees thus, at a glance, the sole methods (sometime indeed absurdly simple ones) by which he may seduce into error or hurry into miscalculation.

Whist has long been known for its influence upon what is termed the calculating power; and men of the highest order of intellect have been known to take an apparently unaccountable delight in it, while eschewing chess as frivolous. Beyond doubt there is nothing of a similar nature so greatly tasking the faculty of analysis. The best chess-player in Christendom *may* be little more than the best player of chess; but proficiency in whist implies capacity for success in all these more important undertakings where mind struggles with mind. When I say proficiency, I mean that perfection in the game which includes a comprehension of *all* the sources whence legitimate advantage may be derived. These are not only manifold, but multiform, and lie frequently among recesses of thought altogether inaccessible to the ordinary understanding. To observe attentively is to remember distinctly; and, so far, the concentrative chess-player will do very well at whist; while the rules of Hoyle (themselves based upon the mere mechanism of the game) are sufficiently and generally comprehensible. Thus to have a retentive memory, and to proceed by "the book" are points commonly regarded as the sum total of good playing. But it is in matters beyond the limits of mere rule that the skill of the analyst is evinced. He makes, in silence, a host of observations and inferences. So, perhaps, do his companions; and the difference in the extent of the information obtained, lies not so much in the validity of the inference as in the quality of the observation. The necessary knowledge is that of *what* to observe. Our player confines himself not at all; nor, because the game is the object, does he reject deductions from things external to the game. He examines the countenance of his partner, comparing it carefully with that of each of his opponents. He considers the mode of assorting the cards in each hand; often counting trump by trump, and honor by honor, through the glances bestowed by their holders upon each. He notes every variation of face as the play progresses, gathering a fund of thought from the differences in the expression of certainty, of surprise, of triumph, or chagrin. From the manner of gathering up a trick he judges whether the person taking it, can make another in the suit. He recognises what is played through feint, by the manner with which it is thrown upon the table. A casual or inadvertent word; the accidental dropping or turning of a card, with the accompanying anxiety or carelessness in regard to its concealment; the counting of the tricks, with the order of their arrangement; embarrassment, hesitation, eagerness, or trepidation—all afford, to his apparently intuitive perception, indications of the true state of affairs. The first two or three rounds having been played, he is in full possession of the contents of each hand, and thenceforward puts down his cards with as absolute a precision of purpose as if the rest of the party had turned outward the faces of their own.

The analytical power should not be confounded with ample ingenuity; for while the analyst is necessarily ingenious, the ingenious man is often remarkably incapable of analysis. The constructive or combining power, by which ingenuity is usually manifested, and to which the phrenologists (I believe erroneously) have assigned a separate organ, supposing it a primitive faculty, has been so frequently seen in those whose intellect bordered otherwise upon idiocy, as to have attracted general observation among writers on morals. Between ingenuity and the analytic ability there exists a difference far greater, indeed, than that between the fancy and the imagination, but of a character very strictly analogous. It will be found, in fact, that the ingenious are always fanciful, and the *truly* imaginative never otherwise than analytic.

The narrative which follows will appear to the reader somewhat in the light of a commentary upon the propositions just advanced.

Residing in Paris during the spring and part of the summer of 18—, I there became acquainted with a Monsieur C. Auguste Dupin. This young gentleman was of an excellent, indeed of an illustrious family, but, by a variety of untoward events, had been reduced to such poverty that the energy of his character succumbed beneath it, and he ceased to bestir himself in the world, or to care for the retrieval of his fortunes. By courtesy of his creditors, there still remained in his possession a small remnant of his patrimony; and, upon the income arising from this, he managed, by means of a rigorous economy, to procure the necessaries of life, without troubling himself about its superfluities. Books, indeed, were his sole luxuries, and in Paris these are easily obtained.

Our first meeting was at an obscure library in the Rue Montmartre, where the accident of our both being in search of the same very rare and very remarkable volume, brought us into closer communion. We saw each other again and again. I was deeply interested in the little family history which he detailed to me with all that candor which a Frenchman indulges whenever mere self is the theme. I was astonished, too, at the vast extent of his reading; and, above all, I felt my soul enkindled within me by the wild fervor, and the vivid freshness of his imagination. Seeking in Paris the objects I then sought, I felt that the society of such a man would be to me a treasure beyond price; and this feeling I frankly confided to him. It was at length arranged that we should live together during my stay in the city; and as my worldly circumstances were somewhat less embarrassed than his own, I was permitted to be at the expense of renting, and furnishing in a style which suited the rather fantastic gloom of our common temper, a time-eaten and grotesque mansion, long deserted through superstitions into which we did not inquire, and tottering to its fall in a retired and desolate portion of the Faubourg St. Germain.

Had the routine of our life at this place been known to the world, we should have been regarded as madmen—although, perhaps, as madmen of a harmless nature. Our seclusion was perfect. We admitted no visitors. Indeed the locality of our retirement had been carefully kept a secret from my own former associates; and it had been many years since Dupin had ceased to know or be known in Paris. We existed within ourselves alone.

It was a freak of fancy in my friend (for what else shall I call it?) to be enamored of the night for her own sake; and into this *bizarrerie*, as into all his

others, I quietly fell; giving myself up to his wild whims with a perfect *abandon*.

The sable divinity would not herself dwell with us always; but we could counter-

feit her presence. At the first dawn of the morning we closed all the messy shut-

ters of our old building; lighted a couple of tapers which, strongly perfumed,

threw out only the ghastliest and feeblest of rays. By the aid of these we then

busied our souls in dreams—reading, writing, or conversing, until warned by the

clock of the advent of the true Darkness. Then we sallied forth into the streets,

arm in arm, continuing the topics of the day, or roaming far and wide until a late

hour, seeking, amid the wild lights and shadows of the populous city, that infin-

ity of mental excitement which quiet observation can afford.

At such times I could not help remarking and admiring (although from his

rich ideality I had been prepared to expect it) a peculiar analytic ability in Dupin.

He seemed, too, to take an eager delight in its exercise—if not exactly in its dis-

play—and did not hesitate to confess the pleasure thus derived. He boasted to

me, with a low chuckling laugh, that most men, in respect to himself, wore win-

dows in their bosoms, and was wont to follow up such assertions by direct and

very startling proofs of his intimate knowledge of my own. His manner at these

moments was frigid and abstract; his eyes were vacant in expression; while his

voice, usually a rich tenor, rose into a treble which would have sounded petulantly but for the deliberateness and entire distinctness of the enunciation. Observing him in these moods, I often dwelt meditatively upon the old philosophy of the Bi-Part Soul, and amused myself with the fancy of a double Dupin—the creative and the resolvent.

Let it not be supposed, from what I have just said, that I am detailing any mystery, or penning any romance. What I have described in the Frenchman was merely the result of an excited, or perhaps of a diseased, intelligence. But of the character of his remarks at the periods in question an example will best convey the idea.

We were strolling one night down a long dirty street, in the vicinity of the Palais Royal. Being both, apparently, occupied with thought, neither of us had spoken a syllable for fifteen minutes at least. All at once Dupin broke forth with these words:

"He is a very little fellow, that's true, and would do better for the *Théâtre des Variétés*."

"There can be no doubt of that," I replied, unwittingly, and not at first observing (so much had I been absorbed in reflection) the extraordinary manner in which the speaker had chimed in with my meditations. In an instant afterward

I recollected myself, and my astonishment was profound.

"Dupin," said I, gravely, "this is beyond my comprehension. I do not hesitate to say that I am amazed, and can scarcely credit my senses. How was it possible you should know I was thinking of——?" Here I paused, to ascertain beyond a doubt whether he really knew of whom I thought.

"——of Chantilly," said he, "why do you pause? You were remarking to yourself that his diminutive figure unfitted him for tragedy."

This was precisely what had formed the subject of my reflections. Chantilly was a *quondam* cobbler of the Rue St. Denis, who, becoming stage-mad, had attempted the *rôle* of Xerxes, in Crébillon's tragedy so called, and been notoriously Pasquinaded for his pains.

"Tell me, for Heaven's sake," I exclaimed, "the method—if method there is—by which you have been enabled to fathom my soul in this matter." In fact, I was even more startled than I would have been willing to express.

"It was the fruiterer," replied my friend, "who brought you to the conclusion that the mender of soles was not of sufficient height for Xerxes *et id genus omne.*"

"The fruiterer!—you astonish me—I know no fruiterer whomsoever."

"The man who ran up against you as we entered the street—it may have been fifteen minutes ago."

I now remembered that, in fact, a fruiterer, carrying upon his head a large basket of apples, had nearly thrown me down, by accident, as we passed from the Rue C—— into the thoroughfare where we stood; but what this had to do with Chantilly I could not possibly understand.

There was not a particle of *charlatânerie* about Dupin. "I will explain," he said, "and that you may comprehend all clearly, we will first retrace the course of your meditations, from the moment in which I spoke to you until that of the *rencontre* with the fruiterer in question. The larger links of the chain run thus—Chantilly, Orion, Dr. Nichols, Epicurus, Stereotomy, the street stones, the fruiterer."

There are few persons who have not, at some period of their lives, amused themselves in retracing the steps by which particular conclusions of their own minds have been attained. The occupation is often full of interest; and he who attempts it for the first time is astonished by the apparently illimitable distance and incoherence between the starting-point and the goal. What, then, must have been my amazement, when I heard the Frenchman speak what he had just spoken, and when I could not help acknowledging that he had spoken the truth. He continued:

"We had been talking of horses, if I remember aright, just before leaving the Rue C——. This was the last subject we discussed. As we crossed into this street, a fruiterer, with a large basket upon his head, brushing quickly past us, thrust you upon a pile of paving-stones collected at a spot where the causeway is undergoing repair. You stepped upon one of the loose fragments, slipped, slightly strained your ankle, appeared vexed or sulky, muttered a few words, turned to look at the pile, and then proceeded in silence. I was not particularly attentive to what you did; but observation has become with me, of late, a species of necessity.

"You kept your eyes upon the ground—glancing, with a petulant expression, at the holes and ruts in the pavement (so that I saw you were still thinking of the stones), until we reached the little alley called Lamartine, which has been paved, by way of experiment, with the overlapping and riveted blocks. Here your countenance brightened up, and, perceiving your lips move, I could not doubt that you murmured the word 'stereotomy,' a term very affectedly applied to this species of pavement. I knew that you could not say to yourself 'stereotomy' without being brought to think of atomies, and thus of the theories of Epicurus; and since, when we discussed this subject not very long ago, I mentioned to you how singularly, yet with how little notice, the vague guesses of that noble Greek had met with confirmation in the late nebular cosmogony, I felt that you could not avoid casting your eyes upward to the great *nebula* in Orion, and I certainly expected that you would do so. You did look up; and I was now assured that I had correctly followed your steps. But in that bitter *tirade* upon Chantilly, which appeared in yesterday's '*Musée*,' the satirist, making some disgraceful allusions to the cobbler's change of name upon assuming the buskin, quoted a Latin line about which we have often conversed. I mean the line

Perdidit antiquum litera prima sonum.

I had told you that this was in reference to Orion, formerly written Urion; and, from certain pungencies connected with this explanation, I was aware that you could not have forgotten it. It was clear, therefore, that you would not fail to combine the two ideas of Orion and Chantilly. That you did combine them I saw by the character of the smile which passed over your lips. You thought of the poor cobbler's immolation. So far, you had been stooping in your gait; but now I saw you draw yourself up to your full height. I was then sure that you reflected upon the diminutive figure of Chantilly. At this point I interrupted your meditations to remark that as, in fact, he *was* a very little fellow—that Chantilly—he would do better at the *Théâtre des Variétés*."

Not long after this, we were looking over an evening edition of the *Gazette des Tribunaux*, when the following paragraphs arrested our attention.

"EXTRAORDINARY MURDERS.—This morning, about three o'clock, the inhabitants of the Quartier St. Roch were roused from sleep by a succession of terrific shrieks, issuing, apparently, from the fourth story of a house in the Rue Morgue, known to be in the sole occupancy of one Madame L'Espanaye, and her daughter, Mademoiselle Camille L'Espanaye. After some delay, occasioned by a fruitless attempt to procure admission in the usual manner, the gateway was broken in with a crowbar, and eight or ten of the neighbors entered, accompanied by two *gendarmes*. By this time the cries had ceased; but, as the party rushed up the first flight of stairs, two or more rough voices, in angry contention, were distinguished, and seemed to proceed from the upper part of the house. As the second landing was reached, these sounds, also, had ceased, and every thing remained perfectly quiet. The party spread themselves, and hurried from room to room. Upon arriving at a large back chamber in the fourth story (the door of which, being found locked, with the key inside, was forced open), a spectacle presented itself which struck every one present not less with horror than with astonishment.

"The apartment was in the wildest disorder—the furniture broken and thrown about in all directions. There was only one bedstead; and from this the bed had been removed, and thrown into the middle of the floor. On a chair lay a razor, besmeared with blood. On the hearth were two or three long and thick

tresses of gray human hair, also dabbled with blood, and seeming to have been pulled out by the roots. Upon the floor were found four Napoleons, an ear-ring of topaz, three large silver spoons, three smaller of *métal d'Alger*, and two bags, containing nearly four thousand francs in gold. The drawers of a *bureau*, which stood in one corner, were open, and had been, apparently, rifled, although many articles still remained in them. A small iron safe was discovered under the *bed* (not under the bedstead). It was open, with the key still in the door. It had no contents beyond a few old letters, and other papers of little consequence.

"Of Madame L'Espanaye no traces were here seen; but an unusual quantity of soot being observed in the fire-place, a search was made in the chimney, and (horrible to relate!) the corpse of the daughter, head downward, was dragged therefrom; it having been thus forced up the narrow aperture for a considerable distance. The body was quite warm. Upon examining it, many excoriations were perceived, no doubt occasioned by the violence with which it had been thrust up and disengaged. Upon the face were many severe scratches, and, upon the throat, dark bruises, and deep indentations of finger nails, as if the deceased had been throttled to death.

"After a thorough investigation of every portion of the house without farther discovery, the party made its way into a small paved yard in the rear of the building, where lay the corpse of the old lady, with her throat so entirely cut that, upon an attempt to raise her, the head fell off. The body, as well as the head, was fearfully mutilated—the former so much so as scarcely to retain any semblance of humanity.

"To this horrible mystery there is not as yet, we believe, the slightest clew."

The next day's paper had these additional particulars.

"*The Tragedy in the Rue Morgue.*—Many individuals have been examined in relation to this most extraordinary and frightful affair," [the word '*affaire*' has not yet, in France, that levity of import which it conveys with us] "but nothing whatever has transpired to throw light upon it. We give below all the material testimony elicited.

"*Pauline Dubourg*, laundress, deposes that she has known both the deceased for three years, having washed for them during that period. The old lady and her daughter seemed on good terms—very affectionate toward each other. They were excellent pay. Could not speak in regard to their mode or means of living. Believed that Madame L. told fortunes for a living. Was reputed to have money put by. Never met any person in the house when she called for the clothes or took them home. Was sure that they had no servant in employ. There appeared to be no furniture in any part of the building except in the fourth story.

"*Pierre Moreau*, tobacconist, deposes that he has been in the habit of selling small quantities of tobacco and snuff to Madame L'Espanaye for nearly four years. Was born in the neighborhood, and has always resided there. The deceased and her daughter had occupied the house in which the corpses were found, for more than six years. It was formerly occupied by a jeweller, who under-let the upper rooms to various persons. The house was the property of Madame L. She became dissatisfied with the abuse of the premises by her tenant, and moved into them herself, refusing to let any portion. The old lady was childish. Witness had seen the daughter some five or six times during the six years. The two lived an exceedingly retired life—were reputed to have money. Had heard it said among the neighbors that Madame L. told fortunes—did not believe it. Had never seen any person enter the door except the old lady and her daughter, a porter once or twice, and a physician some eight or ten times.

"Many other persons, neighbors, gave evidence to the same effect. No one was spoken of as frequenting the house. It was not known whether there were any living connections of Madame L. and her daughter. The shutters of the front windows were seldom opened. Those in the rear were always closed, with the exception of the large back room, fourth story. The house was a good house—not very old.

"*Isidore Musèt, gendarme,* deposes that he was called to the house about three o'clock in the morning, and found some twenty or thirty persons at the gateway, endeavoring to gain admittance. Forced it open, at length, with a bayonet—not with a crowbar. Had but little difficulty in getting it open, on account of its being a double or folding gate, and bolted neither at bottom nor top. The shrieks were continued until the gate was forced—and then suddenly ceased. They seemed to be screams of some person (or persons) in great agony—were loud and drawn out, not short and quick. Witness led the way up stairs. Upon reaching the first landing, heard two voices in loud and angry contention—the one a gruff voice, the other much shriller—a very strange voice. Could distinguish some words of the former, which was that of a Frenchman. Was positive that it was not a woman's voice. Could distinguish the words '*sacré*' and '*diable.*' The shrill voice was that of a foreigner. Could not be sure whether it was the voice of a man or of a woman. Could not make out what was said, but believed the language to be Spanish. The state of the room and of the bodies was described by this witness as we described them yesterday.

"*Henri Duval,* a neighbor, and by trade a silver-smith, deposes that he was one of the party who first entered the house. Corroborates the testimony of Musèt in general. As soon as they forced an entrance, they reclosed the door, to keep out the crowd, which collected very fast, notwithstanding the lateness of the hour. The shrill voice, this witness thinks, was that of an Italian. Was certain it was not French. Could not be sure that it was a man's voice. It might have been a woman's. Was not acquainted with the Italian language. Could not distinguish the words, but was convinced by the intonation that the speaker was an Italian. Knew Madame L. and her daughter. Had conversed with both frequently. Was sure that the shrill voice was not that of either of the deceased.

"——*Odenheimer, restaurateur.*——This witness volunteered his testimony. Not speaking French, was examined through an interpreter. Is a native of Amsterdam. Was passing the house at the time of the shrieks. They lasted for several minutes—probably ten. They were long and loud—very awful and distressing. Was one of those who entered the building. Corroborated the previous evidence in every respect but one. Was sure that the shrill voice was that of a man—of a Frenchman. Could not distinguish the words uttered. They were loud and quick—unequal—spoken apparently in fear as well as in anger. The voice was harsh—not so much shrill as harsh. Could not call it a shrill voice. The gruff voice said repeatedly, 'sacré,' 'diable,' and once 'mon Dieu.'

"*Jules Mignaud*, banker, of the firm of Mignaud et Fils, Rue Deloraine. Is the elder Mignaud. Madame L'Espanaye had some property. Had opened an account

with his banking house in the spring of the year—— (eight years previously).
Made frequent deposits in small sums. Had checked for nothing until the third
day before her death, when she took out in person the sum of 4000 francs. This
sum was paid in gold, and a clerk sent home with the money.

"*Adolphe Le Bon*, clerk to Mignaud et Fils, deposes that on the day in question,
about noon, he accompanied Madame L'Espanaye to her residence with the
4000 francs, put up in two bags. Upon the door being opened, Mademoiselle L.
appeared and took from his hands one of the bags, while the old lady relieved
him of the other. He then bowed and departed. Did not see any person in the
street at the time. It is a by-street—very lonely.

"*William Bird*, tailor, deposes that he was one of the party who entered the
house. Is an Englishman. Has lived in Paris two years. Was one of the first to
ascend the stairs. Heard the voices in contention. The gruff voice was that of a
Frenchman. Could make out several words, but cannot now remember all. Heard
distinctly '*sacré*' and '*mon Dieu.*' There was a sound at the moment as if of several
persons struggling—a scraping and scuffling sound. The shrill voice was very
loud—louder than the gruff one. Is sure that it was not the voice of an Englishman. Appeared to be that of a German. Might have been a woman's voice. Does
not understand German.

"Four of the above-named witnesses, being recalled, deposed that the door of the chamber in which was found the body of Mademoiselle L. was locked on the inside when the party reached it. Every thing was perfectly silent—no groans or noises of any kind. Upon forcing the door no person was seen. The windows, both of the back and front room, were down and firmly fastened from within. A door between the two rooms was closed but not locked. The door leading from the front room into the passage was locked, with the key on the inside. A small room in the front of the house, on the fourth story, at the head of the passage, was open, the door being ajar. This room was crowded with old beds, boxes, and so forth. These were carefully removed and searched. There was not an inch of any portion of the house which was not carefully searched. Sweeps were sent up and down the chimneys. The house was a four-story one, with garrets (*mansardes*). A trap-door on the roof was nailed down very securely—did not appear to have been opened for years. The time elapsing between the hearing of the voices in contention and the breaking open of the room door was variously stated by the witnesses. Some made it as short as three minutes—some as long as five. The door was opened with difficulty.

"*Alfonzo Garcio*, undertaker, deposes that he resides in the Rue Morgue. Is a native of Spain. Was one of the party who entered the house. Did not proceed up stairs. Is nervous, and was apprehensive of the consequences of agitation. Heard the voices in contention. The gruff voice was that of a Frenchman. Could not distinguish what was said. The shrill voice was that of an Englishman—is sure of this. Does not understand the English language, but judges by the intonation.

"*Alberto Montani*, confectioner, deposes that he was among the first to ascend the stairs. Heard the voices in question. The gruff voice was that of a Frenchman. Distinguished several words. The speaker appeared to be expostulating. Could not make out the words of the shrill voice. Spoke quick and unevenly. Thinks it the voice of a Russian. Corroborates the general testimony. Is an Italian. Never conversed with a native of Russia.

"Several witnesses, recalled, here testified that the chimneys of all the rooms on the fourth story were too narrow to admit the passage of a human being. By 'sweeps' were meant cylindrical sweeping-brushes, such as are employed by those who clean chimneys. These brushes were passed up and down every flue in the house. There is no back passage by which any one could have descended while the party proceeded up stairs. The body of Mademoiselle L'Espanaye was so firmly wedged in the chimney that it could not be got down until four or five of the party united their strength.

"*Paul Dumas*, physician, deposes that he was called to view the bodies about daybreak. They were both then lying on the sacking of the bedstead in the chamber where Mademoiselle L. was found. The corpse of the young lady was much bruised and excoriated. The fact that it had been thrust up the chimney would sufficiently account for these appearances. The throat was greatly chafed. There were several deep scratches just below the chin, together with a series of livid spots which were evidently the impression of fingers. The face was fearfully discolored, and the eyeballs protruded. The tongue had been partially bitten through. A large bruise was discovered upon the pit of the stomach, produced, apparently, by the pressure of a knee. In the opinion of M. Dumas, Mademoiselle L'Espanaye had been throttled to death by some person or persons unknown. The corpse of the mother was horribly mutilated. All the bones of the right leg and arm were more or less shattered. The left *tibia* much splintered, as well as all the ribs of the left side. Whole body dreadfully bruised and discolored. It was not possible to say how the injuries had been inflicted. A heavy club of wood, or a broad bar of iron—a chair—any large, heavy, and obtuse weapon would have produced such results, if wielded by the hands of a very powerful man. No woman could have inflicted the blows with any weapon. The head of the deceased, when seen by witness, was entirely separated from the body, and was also greatly shattered. The throat had evidently been cut with some very sharp instrument—probably with a razor.

"*Alexandre Etienne*, surgeon, was called with M. Dumas to view the bodies. Corroborated the testimony, and the opinions of M. Dumas.

"Nothing further of importance was elicited, although several other persons were examined. A murder so mysterious, and so perplexing in all its particulars, was never before committed in Paris—if indeed a murder has been committed at all. The police are entirely at fault—an unusual occurrence in affairs of this nature. There is not, however, the shadow of a clew apparent."

The evening edition of the paper stated that the greatest excitement still continued in the Quartier St. Roch—that the premises in question had been carefully re-searched, and fresh examinations of witnesses instituted, but all to no purpose. A postscript, however, mentioned that Adolphe Le Bon had been arrested and imprisoned—although nothing appeared to criminate him beyond the facts already detailed.

Dupin seemed singularly interested in the progress of this affair—at least so I judged from his manner, for he made no comments. It was only after the announcement that Le Bon had been imprisoned, that he asked me my opinion respecting the murders.

I could merely agree with all Paris in considering them an insoluble mystery. I saw no means by which it would be possible to trace the murderer.

"We must not judge of the means," said Dupin, "by this shell of an examination. The Parisian police, so much extolled for *acumen*, are cunning, but no more. There is no method in their proceedings, beyond the method of the moment. They make a vast parade of measures; but, not unfrequently, these are so ill-adapted to the objects proposed, as to put us in mind of Monsieur Jourdain's calling for his *robe-de-chambre—pour mieux entendre la musique*. The results attained by them are not unfrequently surprising, but, for the most part, are brought about by simple diligence and activity. When these qualities are unavailing, their schemes fail. Vidocq, for example, was a good guesser, and a persevering man. But, without educated thought, he erred continually by the very intensity of his investigations. He impaired his vision by holding the object too close. He might see, perhaps, one or two points with unusual clearness, but in so doing he, necessarily, lost sight of the matter as a whole. Thus there is such a thing as being too profound. Truth is not always in a well. In fact, as regards the more important knowledge, I do believe that she is invariably superficial. The depth lies in the valleys where we seek her, and not upon the mountain-tops where she is found. The modes and sources of this kind of error are well typified in the contemplation of the heavenly bodies. To look at a star by glances—to view it in a side-long way, by turning toward it the exterior portions of the *retina* (more susceptible of feeble impressions of light than the interior), is to behold the star distinctly—is to have the best appreciation of its lustre—a lustre which grows dim just in proportion as we turn our vision *fully* upon it. A greater number of rays actually fall upon the eye in the latter case, but in the former, there is the more refined capacity for comprehension. By undue profundity we perplex and enfeeble thought; and it is possible to make even Venus herself vanish from the firmanent by a scrutiny too sustained, too concentrated, or too direct.

"As for these murders, let us enter into some examinations for ourselves, before we make up an opinion respecting them. An inquiry will afford us amusement," [I thought this an odd term, so applied, but said nothing] "and besides, Le Bon once rendered me a service for which I am not ungrateful. We will go and see the premises with our own eyes. I know G——, the Prefect of Police, and shall have no difficulty in obtaining the necessary permission."

The permission was obtained, and we proceeded at once to the Rue Morgue. This is one of those miserable thoroughfares which intervene between the Rue Richelieu and the Rue St. Roch. It was late in the afternoon when we reached it, as this quarter is at a great distance from that in which we resided. The house was readily found; for there were still many persons gazing up at the closed shutters, with an objectless curiosity, from the opposite side of the way. It was an

ordinary Parisian house, with a gateway, on one side of which was a glazed watch-box, with a sliding panel in the window, indicating a *loge de concierge*. Before going in we walked up the street, turned down an alley, and then, again turning, passed in the rear of the building—Dupin, meanwhile, examining the whole neighbor-hood, as well as the house, with a minuteness of attention for which I could see no possible object.

Retracing our steps, we came again to the front of the dwelling, rang, and, having shown our credentials, were admitted by the agents in charge. We went up stairs—into the chamber where the body of Mademoiselle L'Espanaye had been found, and where both the deceased still lay. The disorders of the room had, as usual, been suffered to exist. I saw nothing beyond what had been stated in the *Gazette des Tribunaux*. Dupin scrutinized every thing—not excepting the bodies of the victims. We then went into the other rooms, and into the yard; a *gendarme* accompanying us throughout. The examination occupied us until dark, when we took our departure. On our way home my companion stepped in for a moment at the office of one of the daily papers.

I have said that the whims of my friend were manifold, and that *Je les ménageais:*—for this phrase there is no English equivalent. It was his humor, now, to decline all conversation on the subject of the murder, until about noon the next day. He then asked me, suddenly, if I had observed any thing *peculiar* at the scene of the atrocity.

There was something in his manner of emphasizing the word "*peculiar*," which caused me to shudder, without knowing why.

"No, nothing *peculiar*," I said; "nothing more, at least, than we both saw stated in the paper."

"The *Gazette*," he replied, "has not entered, I fear, into the unusual horror of the thing. But dismiss the idle opinions of this print. It appears to me that this mystery is considered insoluble, for the very reason which should cause it to be regarded as easy of solution—I mean for the *outré* character of its features. The police are confounded by the seeming absence of motive—not for the murder itself—but for the atrocity of the murder. They are puzzled, too, by the seeming impossibility of reconciling the voices heard in contention, with the facts that no one was discovered upstairs but the assassinated Mademoiselle L'Espanaye, and that there were no means of egress without the notice of the party ascending. The wild disorder of the room; the corpse thrust, with the head downward, up the chimney; the frightful mutilation of the body of the old lady; these considerations, with those just mentioned, and others which I need not mention, have sufficed to paralyze the powers, by putting completely at fault the boasted *acumen*, of the government agents. They have fallen into the gross but common error of confounding the unusual with the abstruse. But it is by these deviations from the plane of the ordinary, that reason feels its way, if at all, in its search for the true. In investigations such as we are now pursuing, it should not be so much asked 'what has occurred,' as 'what has occurred that has never occurred before.' In fact, the facility with which I shall arrive, or have arrived, at the solution of this mystery, is in the direct ratio of its apparent insolubility in the eyes of the police."

I stared at the speaker in mute astonishment.

"I am now awaiting," continued he, looking toward the door of our apartment—"I am now awaiting a person who, although perhaps not the perpetrator of these butcheries, must have been in some measure implicated in their perpetration. Of the worst portion of the crimes committed, it is probable that he is innocent. I hope that I am right in this supposition; for upon it I build my expectation of reading the entire riddle. I look for the man here—in this room—every moment. It is true that he may not arrive; but the probability is that he will. Should he come, it will be necessary to detain him. Here are pistols; and we both know how to use them when occasion demands their use."

I took the pistols, scarcely knowing what I did, or believing what I heard, while Dupin went on, very much as if in a soliloquy. I have already spoken of his abstract manner at such times. His discourse was addressed to myself; but his voice, although by no means loud, had that intonation which is commonly employed in speaking to some one at a great distance. His eyes, vacant in expression, regarded only the wall.

"That the voices heard in contention," he said, "by the party upon the stairs, were not the voices of the women themselves, was fully proved by the evidence. This relieves us of all doubt upon the question whether the old lady could have first destroyed the daughter, and afterward have committed suicide. I speak of this point chiefly for the sake of method; for the strength of Madame L'Espanaye would have been utterly unequal to the task of thrusting her daughter's corpse up the chimney as it was found; and the nature of the wounds upon her own person entirely preclude the idea of self-destruction. Murder, then, has been committed by some third party; and the voices of this third party were those heard in contention. Let me now advert—not to the whole testimony respecting these voices—but to what was *peculiar* in that testimony. Did you observe any thing peculiar about it?"

I remarked that, while all the witnesses agreed in supposing the gruff voice to be that of a Frenchman, there was much disagreement in regard to the shrill, or, as one individual termed it, the harsh voice.

"That was the evidence itself," said Dupin, "but it was not the peculiarity of the evidence. You have observed nothing distinctive. Yet there *was* something to be observed. The witnesses, as you remark, agreed about the gruff voice; they were here unanimous. But in regard to the shrill voice, the peculiarity is—not that they disagreed—but that, while an Italian, an Englishman, a Spaniard, a Hollander, and a Frenchman attempted to describe it, each one spoke of it as that *of a foreigner*. Each is sure that it was not the voice of one of his own countrymen. Each likens it—not to the voice of an individual of any nation with whose language he is conversant—but the converse. The Frenchman supposes it the voice of a Spaniard, and 'might have distinguished some words *had he been acquainted with the Spanish*.' The Dutchman maintains it to have been that of a Frenchman; but we find it stated that '*not understanding French this witness was examined through an interpreter*.' The Englishman thinks it the voice of a German, and '*does not understand German*.' The Spaniard 'is sure' that it was that of an Englishman, but 'judges by the intonation' altogether, '*as he has no knowledge of the English*.' The Italian believes it the voice of a Russian, but '*has never conversed with a native of Russia*.' A second Frenchman differs, moreover, with the first, and is positive that the voice was that of an Italian; but, *not being cognizant of that tongue*, is, like the Spaniard, 'convinced by the intonation.' Now, how strangely unusual must that voice have really been, about which such testimony as this *could* have been elicited!—in whose *tones*, even, denizens of the five great divisions of Europe could recognise nothing familiar! You will say that it might have been the voice of an Asiatic—of an African. Neither Asiatics nor Africans abound in Paris; but, without denying the inference, I will now merely call your attention to three points. The voice is termed by one witness 'harsh rather than shrill.' It is represented by two others to have been 'quick and *unequal*.' No words—no sounds resembling words—were by any witness mentioned as distinguishable.

"I know not," continued Dupin, "what impression I may have made, so far, upon your own understanding; but I do not hesitate to say that legitimate deductions even from this portion of the testimony—the portion respecting the gruff and shrill voices—are in themselves sufficient to engender a suspicion which should give direction to all farther progress in the investigation of the mystery. I said 'legitimate deductions'; but my meaning is not thus fully expressed. I designed to imply that the deductions are the *sole* proper ones, and that the suspicion arises *inevitably* from them as the single result. What the suspicion is, however, I will not say just yet. I merely wish you to bear in mind that, with myself, it was sufficiently forcible to give a definite form—a certain tendency—to my inquiries in the chamber.

"Let us now transport ourselves, in fancy, to this chamber. What shall we first seek here? The means of egress employed by the murderers. It is not too much to say that neither of us believe in præternatural events. Madame and Mademoiselle L'Espanaye were not destroyed by spirits. The doers of the deed were material, and escaped materially. Then how? Fortunately, there is but one mode of reasoning upon the point, and that mode *must* lead us to a definite decision. Let us examine, each by each, the possible means of egress. It is clear that the assassins were in the room where Mademoiselle L'Espanaye was found, or at least in the room adjoining, when the party ascended the stairs. It is then only from these two apartments that we have to seek issues. The police have laid bare the floors, the ceilings, and the masonry of the walls, in every direction. No *secret* issues could have escaped their vigilance. But, not trusting to *their* eyes, I examined with my own. There were, then, *no* secret issues. Both doors leading from the rooms into the passage were securely locked, with the keys inside. Let us turn to the chimneys. These, although of ordinary width for some eight or ten feet above the hearths, will not admit, throughout their extent, the body of a large cat. The impossibility of egress, by means already stated, being thus absolute, we are reduced to the windows. Through those of the front room no one could have escaped without notice from the crowd in the street. The murderers *must* have passed, then, through those of the back room. Now, brought to this conclusion in so unequivocal a manner as we are, it is not our part, as reasoners, to reject it on account of apparent impossibilities. It is only left for us to prove that these apparent 'impossibilities' are, in reality, not such.

"There are two windows in the chamber. One of them is unobstructed by furniture, and is wholly visible. The lower portion of the other is hidden from view by the head of the unwieldy bedstead which is thrust close up against it. The former was found securely fastened from within. It resisted the utmost force of those who endeavored to raise it. A large gimlet-hole had been pierced in its frame to the left, and a very stout nail was found fitted therein, nearly to the head. Upon examining the other window, a similar nail was seen similarly fitted in it; and a vigorous attempt to raise this sash, failed also. The police were now entirely satisfied that egress had not been in these directions. And, *therefore*, it was thought a matter of supererogation to withdraw the nails and open the windows.

"My own examination was somewhat more particular, and was so for the reason I have just given—because here it was, I knew, that all apparent impossibilities *must* be proved to be not such in reality.

"I proceeded to think thus—*a posteriori*. The murderers *did* escape from one of these windows. This being so, they could not have refastened the sashes from the inside, as they were found fastened;—the consideration which put a stop, through its obviousness, to the scrutiny of the police in this quarter. Yet the sashes *were* fastened. They *must*, then, have the power of fastening themselves. There was no escape from this conclusion. I stepped to the unobstructed casement, withdrew the nail with some difficulty, and attempted to raise the sash. It resisted all my efforts, as I had anticipated. A concealed spring must, I now knew, exist; and this corroboration of my idea convinced me that my premises, at least, were correct, however mysterious still appeared the circumstances attending the nails. A careful search soon brought to light the hidden spring. I pressed it, and, satisfied with the discovery, forbore to upraise the sash.

"I now replaced the nail and regarded it attentively. A person passing out through this window might have reclosed it, and the spring would have caught— but the nail could not have been replaced. The conclusion was plain, and again narrowed in the field of my investigations. The assassins *must* have escaped through the other window. Supposing, then, the springs upon each sash to be the same, as was probable, there *must* be found a difference between the nails, or at least between the modes of their fixture. Getting upon the sacking of the bedstead, I looked over the head-board minutely at the second casement. Passing my hand down behind the board, I readily discovered and pressed the spring, which was, as I had supposed, identical in character with its neighbor. I now looked at the nail. It was as stout as the other, and apparently fitted in the same manner—driven in nearly up to the head.

"You will say that I was puzzled; but, if you think so, you must have misunderstood the nature of the inductions. To use a sporting phrase, I had not been once 'at fault.' The scent had never for an instant been lost. There was no flaw in any link of the chain. I had traced the secret to its ultimate result,—and that result was *the nail*. It had, I say, in every respect, the appearance of its fellow in the other window; but this fact was an absolute nullity (conclusive as it might seem to be) when compared with the consideration that here, at this point, terminated the clew. 'There *must* be something wrong,' I said, 'about the nail.' I touched it; and the head, with about a quarter of an inch of the shank, came off in my fingers. The rest of the shank was in the gimlet-hole where it had been broken off. The fracture was an old one (for its edges were incrusted with rust), and had apparently been accomplished by the blow of a hammer, which had partially imbedded, in the top of the bottom sash, the head portion of the nail. I now carefully replaced this head portion in the indentation whence I had taken it, and the resemblance to a perfect nail was complete—the fissure was invisible. Pressing the spring, I gently raised the sash for a few inches; the head went up with it, remaining firm in its bed. I closed the window, and the semblance of the whole nail was again perfect.

"The riddle, so far, was now unriddled. The assassin had escaped through the window which looked upon the bed. Dropping of its own accord upon his exit (or perhaps purposely closed), it had become fastened by the spring; and it was the retention of this spring which had been mistaken by the police for that of the nail,—farther inquiry being thus considered unnecessary.

"The next question is that of the mode of descent. Upon this point I had been satisfied in my walk with you around the building. About five feet and a half from the casement in question there runs a lightning-rod. From this rod it would have been impossible for any one to reach the window itself, to say nothing of entering it. I observed, however, that the shutters of the fourth story were of the peculiar kind called by Parisian carpenters *ferrades*—a kind rarely employed at the present day, but frequently seen upon very old mansions at Lyons and Bour-deaux. They are in the form of an ordinary door (a single, not a folding door), except that the lower half is latticed or worked in open trellis—thus affording an excellent hold for hands. In the present instance these shutters are fully three feet and a half broad. When we saw them from the rear of the house, they were both about half open—that is to say, they stood off at right angles from the wall.

It is probable that the police, as well as myself, examined the back of the tenement; but, if so, in looking at these *ferrades* in the line of their breadth (as they must have done), they did not perceive this great breadth itself, or, at all events, failed to take it into due consideration. In fact, having once satisfied themselves that no egress could have been made in this quarter, they would naturally bestow here a very cursory examination. It was clear to me, however, that the shutter belonging to the window at the head of the bed, would, if swung fully back to the wall, reach to within two feet of the lightning-rod. It was also evident that, by exertion of a very unusual degree of activity and courage, an entrance into the window, from the rod, might have been thus effected. By reaching to the distance of two feet and a half (we now suppose the shutter open to its whole extent) a robber might have taken a firm grasp upon the trellis-work. Letting go, then, his hold upon the rod, placing his feet securely against the wall, and springing boldly from it, he might have swung the shutter so as to close it, and, if we imagine the window open at the time, might even have swung himself into the room.

"I wish you to bear especially in mind that I have spoken of a *very* unusual degree of activity as requisite to success in so hazardous and so difficult a feat. It is my design to show you first, that the thing might possibly have been accomplished:—but, secondly and *chiefly*, I wish to impress upon your understanding the *very extraordinary*—the almost præternatural character of that agility which could have accomplished it.

"You will say, no doubt, using the language of the law, that 'to make out my case,' I should rather undervalue, than insist upon a full estimation of the activity required in this matter. This may be the practice in law, but it is not the usage of reason. My ultimate object is only the truth. My immediate purpose is to lead you to place in juxtaposition, that *very unusual* activity of which I have just spoken, with that *very peculiar* shrill (or harsh) and *unequal* voice, about whose nationality no two persons could be found to agree, and in whose utterance no syllabification could be detected."

At these words a vague and half-formed conception of the meaning of Dupin flitted over my mind. I seemed to be upon the verge of comprehension, without power to comprehend—as men, at times, find themselves upon the brink of remembrance, without being able, in the end, to remember. My friend went on with his discourse.

"You will see," he said, "that I have shifted the question from the mode of egress to that of ingress. It was my design to convey the idea that both were effected in the same manner, at the same point. Let us now revert to the interior of the room. Let us survey the appearances here. The drawers of the bureau, it is said, had been rifled, although many articles of apparel still remained within them. The conclusion here is absurd. It is a mere guess—a very silly one—and no more. How are we to know that the articles found in the drawers were not all these drawers had originally contained? Madame L'Espanaye and her daughter lived an exceedingly retired life—saw no company—seldom went out—had little use for numerous changes of habiliment. Those found were at least of as good quality as any likely to be possessed by these ladies. If a thief had taken any, why did he not take the best—why did he not take all? In a word, why did he abandon four thousand francs in gold to encumber himself with a bundle of linen? The gold *was* abandoned. Nearly the whole sum mentioned by Monsieur Mignaud, the banker, was discovered, in bags, upon the floor. I wish you, therefore, to discard from your thoughts the blundering idea of *motive*, engendered in the brains of the police by that portion of the evidence which speaks of money delivered at the door of the house. Coincidences ten times as remarkable as this (the delivery of the money, and murder committed within three days upon the party receiving it), happen to all of us every hour of our lives, without attracting even momentary notice. Coincidences, in general, are great stumbling-blocks in the way of that class of thinkers who have been educated to know nothing of the theory of probabilities—that theory to which the most glorious objects of human research are indebted for the most glorious of illustration. In the present instance, had the gold been gone, the fact of its delivery three days before would have formed something more than a coincidence. It would have been corroborative of this idea of motive. But, under the real circumstances of the case, if we are to suppose gold the motive of this outrage, we must also imagine the perpetrator so vacillating an idiot as to have abandoned his gold and his motive together.

"Keeping now steadily in mind the points to which I have drawn your attention—that peculiar voice, that unusual agility, and that startling absence of motive in a murder so singularly atrocious as this—let us glance at the butchery itself. Here is a woman strangled to death by manual strength, and thrust up a chimney, head downward. Ordinary assassins employ no such modes of murder as this. Least of all, do they thus dispose of the murdered. In the manner of thrusting the corpse up the chimney, you will admit that there was something *excessively outré*—something altogether irreconcilable with our common notions of human action, even when we suppose the actors the most depraved of men. Think, too, how great must have been that strength which could have thrust the body *up* such an aperture so forcibly that the united vigor of several persons was found barely sufficient to drag it *down!*

"Turn, now, to other indications of the employment of a vigor most marvellous. On the hearth were thick tresses—very thick tresses—of grey human hair. These had been torn out by the roots. You are aware of the great force necessary in tearing thus from the head even twenty or thirty hairs together. You saw the locks in question as well as myself. Their roots (a hideous sight!) were clotted with fragments of the flesh of the scalp—sure token of the prodigious power which had been exerted in uprooting perhaps half a million of hairs at a time. The throat of the old lady was not merely cut, but the head absolutely severed from the body: the instrument was a mere razor. I wish you also to look at the *brutal* ferocity of these deeds. Of the bruises upon the body of Madame L'Espanaye I do not speak. Monsieur Dumas, and his worthy coadjutor Monsieur Etienne, have pronounced that they were inflicted by some obtuse instrument; and so far these gentlemen are very correct. The obtuse instrument was clearly the stone pavement in the yard, upon which the victim had fallen from the window which looked in upon the bed. This idea, however simple it may now seem, escaped the police for the same reason that the breadth of the shutters escaped them—because, by the affair of the nails, their perceptions had been hermetically sealed against the possibility of the windows having ever been opened at all.

"If now, in addition to all these things, you have properly reflected upon the odd disorder of the chamber, we have gone so far as to combine the ideas of an agility astounding, a strength superhuman, a ferocity brutal, a butchery without motive, a *grotesquerie* in horror absolutely alien from humanity, and a voice foreign in tone to the ears of men of many nations, and devoid of all distinct or intelligible syllabification. What result, then, has ensued? What impression have I made upon your fancy?"

I felt a creeping of the flesh as Dupin asked me the question. "A madman," I said, "has done this deed—some raving maniac, escaped from a neighboring *Maison de Santé*."

"In some respects," he replied, "your idea is not irrelevant. But the voices of madmen, even in their wildest paroxysms, are never found to tally with that peculiar voice heard upon the stairs. Madmen are of some nation, and their language, however incoherent in its words, has always the coherence of syllabification. Besides, the hair of a madman is not such as I now hold in my hand. I disentangled this little tuft from the rigidly clutched fingers of Madame L'Espanaye. Tell me what you can make of it."

"Dupin!" I said, completely unnerved; "this hair is most unusual—this is no *human* hair."

"I have not asserted that it is," said he; "but, before we decide this point, I wish you to glance at the little sketch I have here traced upon this paper. It is a *facsimile* drawing of what has been described in one portion of the testimony as 'dark bruises and deep indentations of finger nails' upon the throat of Mademoiselle L'Espanaye, and in another (by Messrs. Dumas and Etienne), as a 'series of livid spots, evidently the impression of fingers.'

"You will perceive," continued my friend, spreading out the paper upon the table before us, "that this drawing gives the idea of a firm and fixed hold. There is no *slipping* apparent. Each finger has retained—possibly until the death of the victim—the fearful grasp by which it originally imbedded itself. Attempt, now, to place all your fingers, at the same time, in the respective impressions as you see them."

I made the attempt in vain.

"We are possibly not giving this matter a fair trial," he said. "The paper is spread out upon a plane surface; but the human throat is cylindrical. Here is a billet of wood, the circumference of which is about that of the throat. Wrap the drawing around it, and try the experiment again."

I did so; but the difficulty was even more obvious than before. "This," I said, "is the mark of no human hand."

"Read now," replied Dupin, "this passage from Cuvier."

It was a minute anatomical and generally descriptive account of the large fulvous Ourang-Outang of the East Indian Islands. The gigantic stature, the prodigious strength and activity, the wild ferocity, and the imitative propensities of these mammalia are sufficiently well known to all. I understood the full horrors of the murder at once.

"The description of the digits," said I, as I made an end of reading, "is in exact accordance with this drawing. I see that no animal but an Ourang-Outang, of the species here mentioned, could have impressed the indentations as you have traced them. This tuft of tawny hair, too, is identical in character with that of the beast of Cuvier. But I cannot possibly comprehend the particulars of this frightful mystery. Besides, there were *two* voices heard in contention, and one of them was unquestionably the voice of a Frenchman."

"True; and you will remember an expression attributed almost unanimously, by the evidence, to this voice,—the expression, '*mon Dieu!*' This, under the circumstances, has been justly characterized by one of the witnesses (Montani, the confectioner) as an expression of remonstrance or expostulation. Upon these two words, therefore, I have mainly built my hopes of a full solution of the riddle. A Frenchman was cognizant of the murder. It is possible—indeed it is far more than probable—that he was innocent of all participation in the bloody transactions which took place. The Ourang-Outang may have escaped from him. He may have traced it to the chamber; but, under the agitating circumstances which ensued, he could never have recaptured it. It is still at large. I will not pursue these guesses—for I have no right to call them more—since the shades of reflection upon which they are based are scarcely of sufficient depth to be appreciable by my own intellect, and since I could not pretend to make them intelligible to the understanding of another. We will call them guesses, then, and speak of them as such. If the Frenchman in question is indeed, as I suppose, innocent of this atrocity, this advertisement, which I left last night, upon our return home, at the office of *Le Monde* (a paper devoted to the shipping interest, and much sought by sailors), will bring him to our residence."

He handed me a paper, and I read thus:

"CAUGHT—*In the Bois de Boulogne, early in the morning of the—inst.* (the morning of the murder), *a very large, tawny Ourang-Outang of the Bornese species. The owner (who is ascertained to be a sailor, belonging to a Maltese vessel) may have the animal again, upon identifying it satisfactorily, and paying a few charges arising from its capture and keeping. Call at No.——, Rue——, Faubourg St. Germain—au troisième.*"

"How was it possible," I asked, "that you should know the man to be a sailor, and belonging to a Maltese vessel?"

"I do *not* know it," said Dupin. "I am not *sure* of it. Here, however, is a small piece of ribbon, which from its form, and from its greasy appearance, has evidently been used in tying the hair in one of those long *queues* of which sailors are so fond. Moreover, this knot is one which few besides sailors can tie, and is peculiar to the Maltese. I picked the ribbon up at the foot of the lightning-rod. It could not have belonged to either of the deceased. Now if, after all, I am wrong in my induction from this ribbon, that the Frenchman was a sailor belonging to a Maltese vessel, still I can have done no harm in saying what I did in the advertisement. If I am in error, he will merely suppose that I have been misled by some circumstance into which he will not take the trouble to inquire. But if I am right, a great point is gained. Cognizant although innocent of the murder, the Frenchman will naturally hesitate about replying to the advertisement—about demanding the Ourang-Outang. He will reason thus:—'I am innocent; I am poor; my Ourang-Outang is of great value—to one in my circumstances a fortune of itself—why should I lose it through idle apprehensions of danger? Here it is, within my grasp. It was found in the Bois de Boulogne—at a vast distance from the scene of that butchery. How can it ever be suspected that a brute beast should have done the deed? The police are at fault—they have failed to procure the slightest clew. Should they even trace the animal, it would be impossible to prove me cognizant of the murder, or to implicate me in guilt on account of that cognizance. Above all, *I am known*. The advertiser designates me as the possessor of the beast. I am not sure to what limit his knowledge may extend. Should I avoid claiming a property of so great value, which it is known that I possess, I will render the animal at least, liable to suspicion. It is not my policy to attract attention either to myself or to the beast. I will answer the advertisement, get the Ourang-Outang, and keep it close until this matter has blown over.'"

At this moment we heard a step upon the stairs.

"Be ready," said Dupin, "with your pistols, but neither use them nor show them until at a signal from myself."

The front door of the house had been left open, and the visitor had entered, without ringing, and advanced several steps upon the staircase. Now, however, he seemed to hesitate. Presently we heard him descending. Dupin was moving quickly to the door, when we again heard him coming up. He did not turn back a second time, but stepped up with decision, and rapped at the door of our chamber.

"Come in," said Dupin, in a cheerful and hearty tone.

A man entered. He was a sailor, evidently,—a tall, stout, and muscular-looking person, with a certain dare devil expression of countenance, not altogether unprepossessing. His face, greatly sunburnt, was more than half hidden by whisker and *mustachio*. He had with him a huge oaken cudgel, but appeared to be otherwise unarmed. He bowed awkwardly, and bade us "good evening," in French accents, which, although somewhat Neufchatelish, were still sufficiently indicative of a Parisian origin.

"Sit down, my friend," said Dupin. "I suppose you have called about the Ourang-Outang. Upon my word, I almost envy you the possession of him; a remarkably fine, and no doubt a very valuable animal. How old do you suppose him to be?"

The sailor drew a long breath, with the air of a man relieved of some intolerable burden, and then replied, in an assured tone:

"I have no way of telling—but he can't be more than four or five years old. Have you got him here?"

"Oh, no; we had no conveniences for keeping him here. He is at a livery stable in the Rue Dubourg, just by. You can get him in the morning. Of course you are prepared to identify the property?"

"To be sure I am, sir."

"I shall be sorry to part with him," said Dupin.

"I don't mean that you should be at all this trouble for nothing, sir," said the man. "Couldn't expect it. Am very willing to pay a reward for the finding of the animal—that is to say, any thing in reason."

"Well," replied my friend, "that is all very fair, to be sure. Let me think!—what should I have? Oh! I will tell you. My reward shall be this. You shall give me all the information in your power about these murders in the Rue Morgue."

Dupin said the last words in a very low tone, and very quietly. Just as quietly, too, he walked toward the door, locked it, and put the key in his pocket. He then drew a pistol from his bosom and placed it, without the least flurry, upon the table.

The sailor's face flushed up as if he were struggling with suffocation. He started to his feet and grasped his cudgel, but the next moment he fell back into his seat, trembling violently, and with the countenance of death itself. He spoke not a word. I pitied him from the bottom of my heart.

"My friend," said Dupin, in a kind tone, "you are alarming yourself unnecessarily—you are indeed. We mean you no harm whatever. I pledge you the honor of a gentleman, and of a Frenchman, that we intend you no injury. I perfectly well know that you are innocent of the atrocities in the Rue Morgue. It will not do, however, to deny that you are in some measure implicated in them. From what I have already said, you must know that I have had means of information about this matter—means of which you could never have dreamed. Now the thing stands thus. You have done nothing which you could have avoided—nothing, certainly, which renders you culpable. You were not even guilty of robbery, when you might have robbed with impunity. You have nothing to conceal. You have no reason for concealment. On the other hand, you are bound by every principle of honor to confess all you know. An innocent man is now imprisoned, charged with that crime of which you can point out the perpetrator."

The sailor had recovered his presence of mind, in a great measure, while Dupin uttered these words; but his original boldness of bearing was all gone.

"So help me God!" said he, after a brief pause, "I *will* tell you all I know about this affair;—but I do not expect you to believe one half I say—I would be a fool indeed if I did. Still, I *am* innocent, and I will make a clean breast if I die for it."

What he stated was, in substance, this. He had lately made a voyage to the Indian Archipelago. A party, of which he formed one, landed at Borneo, and passed into the interior on an excursion of pleasure. Himself and a companion had captured the Ourang-Outang. This companion dying, the animal fell into his own exclusive possession. After great trouble, occasioned by the intractable ferocity of his captive during the home voyage, he at length succeeded in lodging it safely at his own residence in Paris, where, not to attract toward himself the unpleasant curiosity of his neighbors, he kept it carefully secluded, until such time as it should recover from a wound in the foot, received from a splinter on board ship. His ultimate design was to sell it.

Returning home from some sailors' frolic the night, or rather in the morning of the murder, he found the beast occupying his own bedroom, into which it had broken from a closet adjoining, where it had been, as was thought, securely confined. Razor in hand, and fully lathered, it was sitting before a looking-glass, attempting the operation of shaving, in which it had no doubt previously watched its master through the key-hole of the closet. Terrified at the sight of so dangerous a weapon in the possession of an animal so ferocious, and so well able to use it, the man, for some moments, was at a loss what to do. He had been accustomed, however, to quiet the creature, even in its fiercest moods, by the use of a whip, and to this he now resorted. Upon sight of it, the Ourang-Outang sprang at once through the door of the chamber, down the stairs, and thence, through a window, unfortunately open, into the street.

The Frenchman followed in despair; the ape, razor still in hand, occasionally stopping to look back and gesticulate at his pursuer, until the latter had nearly come up with it. It then again made off. In this manner the chase continued for a long time. The streets were profoundly quiet, as it was nearly three o'clock in

the morning. In passing down an alley in the rear of the Rue Morgue, the fugitive's attention was arrested by a light gleaming from the open window of Madame L'Espanaye's chamber, in the fourth story of her house. Rushing to the building, it perceived the lightning-rod, clambered up with inconceivable agility, grasped the shutter, which was thrown fully back against the wall, and, by its means, swung itself directly upon the headboard of the bed. The whole feat did not occupy a minute. The shutter was kicked open again by the Ourang-Outang as it entered the room.

The sailor, in the meantime, was both rejoiced and perplexed. He had strong hopes of now recapturing the brute, as it could scarcely escape from the trap into which it had ventured, except by the rod, where it might be intercepted as it came down. On the other hand, there was much cause for anxiety as to what it might do in the house. This latter reflection urged the man still to follow the fugitive. A lightning-rod is ascended without difficulty, especially by a sailor; but, when he had arrived as high as the window, which lay far to his left, his career was stopped; the most that he could accomplish was to reach over so as to obtain a glimpse of the interior of the room. At this glimpse he nearly fell from his hold through excess of horror. Now it was that those hideous shrieks arose upon the night, which had startled from slumber the inmates of the Rue Morgue. Madame

L'Espanaye and her daughter, habited in their night clothes, had apparently been occupied in arranging some papers in the iron chest already mentioned, which had been wheeled into the middle of the room. It was open, and its contents lay beside it on the floor. The victims must have been sitting with their backs toward the window; and, from the time elapsing between the ingress of the beast and the screams, it seems probable that it was not immediately perceived. The flapping-to of the shutter would naturally have been attributed to the wind.

As the sailor looked in, the gigantic animal had seized Madame L'Espanaye by the hair (which was loose, as she had been combing it), and was flourishing the razor about her face, in imitation of the motions of a barber. The daughter lay prostrate and motionless; she had swooned. The screams and struggles of the old lady (during which the hair was torn from her head) had the effect of changing the probably pacific purposes of the Ourang-Outang into those of wrath. With one determined sweep of its muscular arm it nearly severed her head from her body. The sight of blood inflamed its anger into phrenzy. Gnashing its teeth, and flashing fire from its eyes, it flew upon the body of the girl, and imbedded its fearful talons in her throat, retaining its grasp until she expired. Its wandering and wild glances fell at this moment upon the head of the bed, over which the face of its master, rigid with horror, was just discernible. The fury of the beast, who no doubt bore still in mind the dreaded whip, was instantly converted into fear. Conscious of having deserved punishment, it seemed desirous of concealing its bloody deeds, and skipped about the chamber in an agony of nervous agitation; throwing down and breaking the furniture as it moved, and dragging the bed from the bedstead. In conclusion, it seized first the corpse of the daughter, and thrust it up the chimney, as it was found; then that of the old lady, which it immediately hurled through the window headlong.

As the ape approached the casement with its mutilated burden, the sailor shrank aghast to the rod, and, rather gliding than clambering down it, hurried at once home—dreading the consequences of the butchery, and gladly abandoning, in his terror, all solicitude about the fate of the Ourang-Outang. The words heard by the party upon the staircase were the Frenchman's exclamations of horror and affright, commingled with the fiendish jabberings of the brute.

I have scarcely any thing to add. The Ourang-Outang must have escaped from the chamber, by the rod, just before the break of the door. It must have closed the window as it passed through it. It was subsequently caught by the owner himself, who obtained for it a very large sum at the *Jardin des Plantes.* Le Bon was instantly released, upon our narration of the circumstances (with some comments from Dupin) at the bureau of the Prefect of Police. This functionary, however well disposed to my friend, could not altogether conceal his chagrin at the turn which affairs had taken, and was fain to indulge in a sarcasm or two, about the propriety of every person minding his own business.

"Let him talk," said Dupin, who had not thought it necessary to reply. "Let him discourse; it will ease his conscience, I am satisfied with having defeated him in his own castle. Nevertheless, that he failed in the solution of this mystery, is by no means that matter for wonder which he supposes it; for, in truth, our friend the Prefect is somewhat too cunning to be profound. In his wisdom is no *stamen*. It is all head and no body, like the pictures of the Goddess Laverna—or, at best, all head and shoulders, like a codfish. But he is a good creature after all. I like him especially for one master stroke of cant, by which he has attained his reputation for ingenuity. I mean the way he has '*de nier ce qui est, et d'expliquer ce qui n'est pas.*'"

The Balloon-Hoax

[Astounding News by Express, via Norfolk!—The Atlantic crossed in Three Days! Signal Triumph of Mr. Monck Mason's Flying Machine!—Arrival at Sullivan's Island, near Charlestown, S.C., of Mr. Mason, Mr. Robert Holland, Mr. Henson, Mr. Harrison Ainsworth, and four others, in the Steering Balloon, "Victoria," after a passage of Seventy-five Hours from Land to Land! Full Particulars of the Voyage!

The subjoined jeu d'esprit *with the preceding heading in magnificent capitals, well interspersed with notes of admiration, was originally published, as matter of fact, in the* New-York Sun, *a daily newspaper, and therein "fully subserved the purpose of creating indigestible aliment for the* quidnuncs *during the few hours intervening between a couple of the Charleston mails. The rush for the "sole paper which had the news," was something beyond even the prodigious; and, in fact, if (as some assert) the "Victoria" did not absolutely accomplish the voyage recorded, it will be difficult to assign a reason why she should not have accomplished it.]*

THE great problem is at length solved! The air, as well as the earth and the ocean, has been subdued by science, and will become a common and convenient highway for mankind. *The Atlantic has been actually crossed in a Balloon!* and this too without difficulty—without any great apparent danger—with thorough control of the machine—and in the inconceivably brief period of seventy-five hours from shore to shore! By the energy of an agent at Charleston, S.C., we are enabled to be the first to furnish the public with a detailed account of this most extraordinary voyage, which was performed between Saturday, the 6th instant, at 11 A.M. and 2 P.M., on Tuesday, the 9th instant, by Sir Everard Bringhurst; Mr. Osborne, a nephew of Lord Bentinck's; Mr. Monck Mason and Mr. Robert Holland, the well-known aëronauts; Mr. Harrison Ainsworth, author of "Jack Sheppard," etc.; and Mr. Henson, the projector of the late unsuccessful flying machine—with two seamen from Woolwich—in all, eight persons. The particulars furnished below may be relied on as authentic and accurate in every respect, as, with a slight exception, they are copied *verbatim* from the joint diaries of Mr. Monck Mason and Mr. Harrison Ainsworth, to whose politeness our agent is also indebted for much verbal information respecting the balloon itself, its construction, and other matters of interest. The only alteration in the MS. received, has been made for the purpose of throwing the hurried account of our agent, Mr. Forsyth, into a connected and intelligible form.

"THE BALLOON.

"Two very decided failures, of late—those of Mr. Henson and Sir George Cayley,—had much weakened the public interest in the subject of aërial navigation. Mr. Henson's scheme (which at first was considered very feasible even by men of science) was founded upon the principle of an inclined plane, started from an eminence by an extrinsic force, applied and continued by the revolution of impinging vanes, in form and number resembling the vanes of a windmill. But, in all the experiments made with models at the Adelaide Gallery, it was found that the operation of these fans not only did not propel the machine, but actually impeded its flight. The only propelling force it ever exhibited, was the mere *impetus* acquired from the descent of the inclined plane; and this *impetus* carried the machine farther when the vanes were at rest, than when they were in motion—a fact which sufficiently demonstrates their inutility; and in the absence of the propelling, which was also the *sustaining*, power, the whole fabric would necessarily descend. This consideration led Sir George Cayley to think only of adapting a propeller to some machine having of itself an independent power of support—in a word, to a balloon; the idea, however, being novel, or original, with Sir George, only so far as regards the mode of its application to practice. He exhibited a model of his invention at the Polytechnic Institution. The propelling principle, or power, was here, also, applied to interrupted surfaces, or vanes, put in revolution. These vanes were four in number, but were found entirely ineffectual in moving the balloon, or in aiding its ascending power. The whole project was thus a complete failure.

"It was at this juncture that Mr. Monck Mason (whose voyage from Dover to Weilburg in the balloon, 'Nassau,' occasioned so much excitement in 1837) conceived the idea of employing the principle of the Archimedean screw for the purpose of propulsion through the air—rightly attributing the failure of Mr. Henson's scheme, and of Sir George Cayley's, to the interruption of surface in the independent vanes. He made the first public experiment at Willis's Rooms, but afterward removed his model to the Adelaide Gallery.

"Like Sir George Cayley's balloon, his own was an ellipsoid. Its length was thirteen feet six inches—height, six feet eight inches. It contained about three hundred and twenty cubic feet of gas, which, if pure hydrogen, would support twenty-one pounds upon its first inflation, before the gas has time to deteriorate or escape. The weight of the whole machine and apparatus was seventeen pounds—leaving about four pounds to spare. Beneath the centre of the balloon, was a frame of light wood, about nine feet long, and rigged on to the balloon

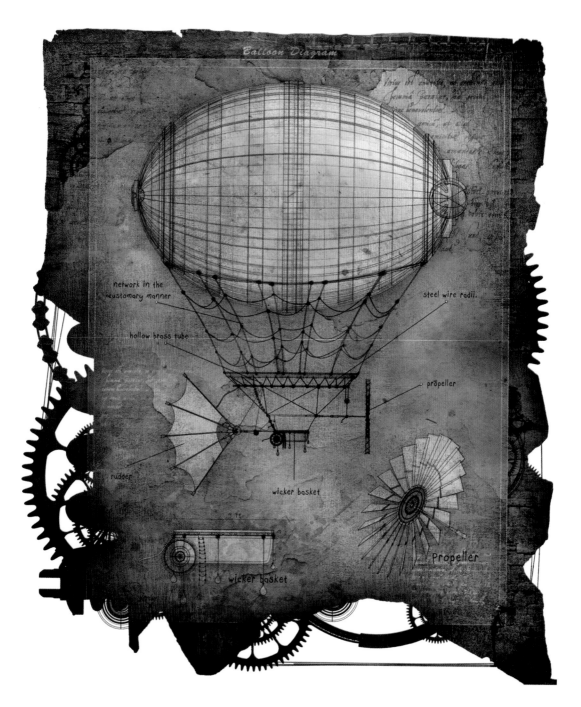

Balloon Diagram

network in the
customary manner

steel wire radii.

hollow brass tube

propeller

rudder

wicker basket

9 ft

wicker basket

Propeller

itself with a network in the customary manner. From this framework was suspended a wicker basket or car.

"The screw consists of an axis of hollow brass tube, eighteen inches in length, through which, upon a semi-spiral inclined at fifteen degrees, pass a series of steel-wire radii, two feet long, and thus projecting a foot on either side. These radii are connected at the outer extremities by two bands of flattened wire—the whole in this manner forming the framework of the screw, which is completed by a covering of oiled silk cut into gores, and tightened so as to present a tolerably uniform surface. At each end of its axis this screw is supported by pillars of hollow brass tube descending from the hoop. In the lower ends of these tubes are holes in which the pivots of the axis revolve. From the end of the axis which is next the car, proceeds a shaft of steel, connecting the screw with the pinion of a piece of spring machinery fixed in the car. By the operation of this spring, the screw is made to revolve with great rapidity, communicating a progressive motion to the whole. By means of the rudder, the machine was readily turned in any direction. The spring was of great power, compared with its dimensions, being capable of raising forty-five pounds upon a barrel of four inches diameter, after the first turn, and gradually increasing as it was wound up. It weighed, altogether, eight pounds six ounces. The rudder was a light frame of cane covered with silk, shaped somewhat like a battledoor, and was about three feet long, and at the widest, one foot. Its weight was about two ounces. It could be turned *flat*, and directed upward or downward, as well as to the right or left; and thus enabled the aëronaut to transfer the resistance of the air which in an inclined position it must generate in its passage, to any side upon which he might desire to act; thus determining the balloon in the opposite direction.

"This model (which, through want of time, we have necessarily described in an imperfect manner) was put in action at the Adelaide Gallery, where it accomplished a velocity of five miles per hour; although, strange to say, it excited very little interest in comparison with the previous complex machine of Mr. Henson—so resolute is the world to despise any thing which carries with it an air of simplicity. To accomplish the great desideratum of aërial navigation, it was very generally supposed that some exceedingly complicated application must be made of some unusually profound principle in dynamics.

"So well satisfied, however, was Mr. Mason of the ultimate success of his invention, that he determined to construct immediately, if possible, a balloon of sufficient capacity to test the question by a voyage of some extent—the original design being to cross the British Channel, as before, in the Nassau balloon. To carry out his views, he solicited and obtained the patronage of Sir Everard

Bringhurst and Mr. Osborne, two gentlemen well known for scientific acquire-
ment, and especially for the interest they have exhibited in the progress of
aërostation. The project, at the desire of Mr. Osborne, was kept a profound
secret from the public—the only persons entrusted with the design being those
actually engaged in the construction of the machine, which was built (under the
superintendence of Mr. Mason, Mr. Holland, Sir Everard Bringhurst, and
Mr. Osborne) at the seat of the latter gentleman near Penstruthal, in Wales. Mr.
Henson, accompanied by his friend Mr. Ainsworth, was admitted to a private
view of the balloon, on Saturday last—when the two gentlemen made final
arrangements to be included in the adventure. We are not informed for what
reason the two seamen were also included in the party—but, in the course of a
day or two, we shall put our readers in possession of the minutest particulars
respecting this extraordinary voyage.

"The balloon is composed of silk, varnished with the liquid gum caoutchouc.
It is of vast dimensions, containing more than 40,000 cubic feet of gas; but as
coal-gas was employed in place of the more expensive and inconvenient hydrogen, the supporting power of the machine, when fully inflated, and immediately
after inflation, is not more than about 2500 pounds. The coal-gas is not only
much less costly, but is easily procured and managed.

"For its introduction into common use for purposes of aërostation, we are indebted to Mr. Charles Green. Up to his discovery, the process of inflation was not only exceedingly expensive, but uncertain. Two and even three days have frequently been wasted in futile attempts to procure a sufficiency of hydrogen to fill a balloon, from which it had great tendency to escape, owing to its extreme subtlety, and its affinity for the surrounding atmosphere. In a balloon sufficiently perfect to retain its contents of coal-gas unaltered, in quantity or amount, for six months, an equal quantity of hydrogen could not be maintained in equal purity for six weeks.

"The supporting power being estimated at 2500 pounds, and the united weights of the party amounting only to about 1200, there was left a surplus of 1300, of which again 1200 was exhausted by ballast, arranged in bags of different sizes, with their respective weights marked upon them—by cordage, barometers, telescopes, barrels containing provision for a fortnight, water-casks, cloaks, carpet-bags, and various other indispensable matters, including a coffee-warmer, contrived for warming coffee by means of slack-lime, so as to dispense altogether with fire, if it should be judged prudent to do so. All these articles, with the exception of the ballast, and a few trifles, were suspended from the hoop overhead. The car is much smaller and lighter, in proportion, than the one appended to the model. It is formed of a light wicker, and is wonderfully strong, for so frail-looking a machine. Its rim is about four feet deep. The rudder is also very much larger, in proportion, than that of the model; and the screw is considerably smaller. The balloon is furnished besides with a grapnel, and a guide-rope; which latter is of the most indispensable importance. A few words, in explanation, will here be necessary for such of our readers as are not conversant with the details of aërostation.

"As soon as the balloon quits the earth, it is subjected to the influence of many circumstances tending to create a difference in its weight; augmenting or diminishing its ascending power. For example, there may be a deposition of dew upon the silk, to the extent, even, of several hundred pounds; ballast has then to be thrown out, or the machine may descend. This ballast being discarded, and a clear sunshine evaporating the dew, and at the same time expanding the gas in the silk, the whole will again rapidly ascend. To check this ascent, the only recourse is (or rather *was*, until Mr. Green's invention of the guide-rope) the permission of the escape of gas from the valve; but, in the loss of gas, is a proportionate general loss of ascending power; so that, in a comparatively brief period, the best-constructed balloon must necessarily exhaust all its resources, and come to the earth. This was the great obstacle to voyages of length.

"The guide-rope remedies the difficulty in the simplest manner conceivable. It is merely a very long rope which is suffered to trail from the car, and the effect of which is to prevent the balloon from changing its level in any material degree. If, for example, there should be a deposition of moisture upon the silk, and the machine begins to descend in consequence, there will be no necessity for discharging ballast to remedy the increase of weight, for it is remedied, or counteracted, in an exactly just proportion, by the deposit on the ground of just so much of the end of the rope as is necessary. If, on the other hand, any circumstances should cause undue levity, and consequent ascent, this levity is immediately counteracted by the additional weight of rope upraised from the earth. Thus, the balloon can neither ascend or descend, except within very narrow limits, and its resources, either in gas or ballast, remain comparatively unimpaired. When passing over an expanse of water, it becomes necessary to employ small kegs of copper or wood, filled with liquid ballast of a lighter nature than water. These float, and serve all the purposes of a mere rope on land. Another most important office of the guide-rope, is to point out the *direction* of the balloon. The rope *drags*, either on land or sea, while the balloon is free; the latter, consequently, is always in advance, when any progress whatever is made; a comparison, therefore, by means of the compass, of the relative positions of the two objects, will always indicate the *course*. In the same way, the angle formed by the rope with the vertical axis of the machine, indicates the *velocity*. When there is *no* angle—in other words, when the rope hangs perpendicularly, the whole apparatus is stationary; but the larger the angle, that is to say, the farther the balloon precedes the end of the rope, the greater the velocity; and the converse.

"As the original design was to cross the British Channel, and alight as near Paris as possible, the voyagers had taken the precaution to prepare themselves with passports directed to all parts of the Continent, specifying the nature of the expedition, as in the case of the 'Nassau' voyage, and entitling the adventurers to exemption from the usual formalities of office; unexpected events, however, rendered these passports superfluous.

"The inflation was commenced very quietly at daybreak, on Saturday morning, the 6th instant, in the courtyard of Wheal-Vor House, Mr. Osborne's seat, about a mile from Penstruthal, in North Wales; and at seven minutes past eleven, every thing being ready for departure, the balloon was set free, rising gently but steadily, in a direction nearly south; no use being made, for the first half hour, of either the screw or the rudder. We proceed now with the journal, as transcribed by Mr. Forsyth from the joint MSS. of Mr. Monck Mason and Mr. Ainsworth. The body of the journal, as given, is in the handwriting of Mr. Mason, and a

P. S. is appended, each day, by Mr. Ainsworth, who has in preparation, and will shortly give the public a more minute, and no doubt, a thrillingly interesting account of the voyage.

"THE JOURNAL.

"*Saturday, April the 6th.*—Every preparation likely to embarrass us, having been made overnight, we commenced the inflation this morning at daybreak; but owing to a thick fog, which encumbered the folds of the silk and rendered it unmanageable, we did not get through before nearly eleven o'clock. Cut loose, then, in high spirits, and rose gently but steadily, with a light breeze at north, which bore us in the direction of the British Channel. Found the ascending force greater than we had expected; and as we arose higher and so got clear of the cliffs, and more in the sun's rays, our ascent became very rapid. I did not wish, however, to lose gas at so early a period of the adventure, and so concluded to ascend for the present. We soon ran out our guide-rope; but even when we had raised it clear of the earth, we still went up very rapidly. The balloon was unusually steady, and looked beautifully. In about ten minutes after starting, the barometer indicated an altitude of 15,000 feet. The weather was remarkably fine, and the view of the subjacent country—a most romantic one when seen

from any point—was now especially sublime. The numerous deep gorges presented the appearance of lakes, on account of the dense vapors with which they were filled, and the pinnacles and crags to the south east, piled in inextricable confusion, resembling nothing so much as the giant cities of Eastern fable. We were rapidly approaching the mountains in the south, but our elevation was more than sufficient to enable us to pass them in safety. In a few minutes we soared over them in fine style; and Mr. Ainsworth, with the seamen, was surprised at their apparent want of altitude when viewed from the car, the tendency of great elevation in a balloon being to reduce inequalities of the surface below, to nearly a dead level. At half-past eleven still proceeding nearly south, we obtained our first view of the Bristol Channel; and, in fifteen minutes afterward, the line of breakers on the coast appeared immediately beneath us, and we were fairly out at sea. We now resolved to let off enough gas to bring our guide-rope, with the buoys affixed, into the water. This was immediately done, and we commenced a gradual descent. In about twenty minutes our first buoy dipped, and at the touch of the second soon afterward, we remained stationary as to elevation. We were all now anxious to test the efficiency of the rudder and screw, and we put them both into requisition forthwith, for the purpose of altering our direction more to the eastward, and in a line for Paris. By means of the rudder we instantly effected the necessary change of direction, and our course was brought nearly at right angles to that of the wind; when we set in motion the spring of the screw, and were rejoiced to find it propel us readily as desired. Upon this we gave nine hearty cheers, and dropped in the sea a bottle, enclosing a slip of parchment with a brief account of the principle of the invention. Hardly, however, had we done with our rejoicings, when an unforeseen accident occurred which discouraged us in no little degree. The steel rod connecting the spring with the propeller was suddenly jerked out of place, at the car end (by a swaying of the car through some movement of one of the two seamen we had taken up), and in an instant hung dangling out of reach, from the pivot of the axis of the screw. While we were endeavoring to regain it, our attention being completely absorbed, we became involved in a strong current of wind from the east, which bore us, with rapidly increasing force, toward the Atlantic. We soon found ourselves driving out to sea at the rate of not less, certainly, than fifty or sixty miles an hour, so that we came up with Cape Clear, at some forty miles to our north, before we had secured the rod, and had time to think what we were about. It was now that Mr. Ainsworth made an extraordinary, but to my fancy, a by no means unreasonable or chimerical proposition, in which he was instantly seconded by Mr. Holland—viz.: that we should take advantage of the strong gale which bore us on, and in place of beating back to Paris, make an attempt to reach the coast of North America. After slight reflection I gave a willing assent to this bold proposition, which (strange to say) met with objection from the two seamen only. As the stronger party, however, we overruled their fears, and kept resolutely upon our course. We steered due west; but as the trailing of the buoys materially impeded our progress, and we had the balloon abundantly at command, either for ascent or descent, we first threw out fifty pounds of ballast, and then wound up (by means of a windlass) so much of the rope as brought it quite clear of the sea. We perceived the effect of this manœuvre immediately, in a vastly increased rate of progress; and, as the gale freshened, we flew with a velocity nearly inconceivable; the guide-rope flying out behind the car, like a streamer from a vessel. It is needless to say that a very short time sufficed us to lose sight of the coast. We passed over innumerable vessels of all kinds, a few of which were endeavoring to beat up, but the most of them lying to. We occasioned the greatest excitement on board all—an excitement greatly relished by ourselves, and especially by our two men, who, now under the influence of a dram of Geneva, seemed resolved to give all scruple, or fear, to the wind. Many of the vessels fired signal guns; and in all we were saluted with loud cheers (which we heard with surprising distinctness) and the waving of caps and handkerchiefs. We kept on in this manner throughout the day with no material incident, and, as the shades of night closed around us, we made a rough estimate of the distance traversed. It could not have been less than five hundred miles, and was probably much more. The propeller was kept in constant operation, and, no doubt, aided our progress materially. As the sun went down, the gale freshened into an absolute hurricane, and the ocean beneath was clearly visible on account of its phosphorescence. The wind was from the east all night, and gave us the brightest omen of success. We suffered no little from cold, and the dampness of the atmosphere was most unpleasant; but the ample space in the car enabled us to lie down, and by means of cloaks and a few blankets we did sufficiently well.

"P.S. [by Mr. Ainsworth] The last nine hours have been unquestionably the most exciting of my life. I can conceive nothing more sublimating than the strange peril and novelty of an adventure such as this. May God grant that we succeed! I ask not success for mere safety to my insignificant person, but for the sake of human knowledge and—for the vastness of the triumph. And yet the feat is only so evidently feasible that the sole wonder is why men have scrupled to attempt it before. One single gale such as now befriends us—let such a tempest whirl forward a balloon for four or five days (these gales often last longer) and the voyager will be easily borne, in that period, from coast to coast. In view of

such a gale the broad Atlantic becomes a mere lake. I am more struck, just now, with the supreme silence which reigns in the sea beneath us, notwithstanding its agitation, than with any other phenomenon presenting itself. The waters give up no voice to the heavens. The immense flaming ocean writhes and is tortured uncomplainingly. The mountainous surges suggest the idea of innumerable dumb gigantic fiends struggling in impotent agony. In a night such as is this to me, a man *lives*—lives a whole century of ordinary life—nor would I forego this rapturous delight for that of a whole century of ordinary existence.

"*Sunday, the 7th.* [Mr. Mason's MS.] This morning the gale, by ten, had sub-sided to an eight- or nine-knot breeze (for a vessel at sea) and bears us, perhaps, thirty miles per hour, or more. It has veered, however, very considerably to the north; and now, at sundown, we are holding our course due west, principally by the screw and rudder, which answer their purposes to admiration. I regard the project as thoroughly successful, and the easy navigation of the air in any direc-tion (not exactly in the teeth of a gale) as no longer problematical. We could not have made head against the strong wind of yesterday; but, by ascending, we might have got out of its influence, if requisite. Against a pretty stiff breeze, I feel con-vinced, we can make our way with the propeller. At noon, to-day, ascended to an elevation of nearly 25,000 feet, by discharging ballast. Did this to search for a more direct current, but found none so favorable as the one we are now in. We have an abundance of gas to take us across this small pond, even should the voyage last three weeks. I have not the slightest fear for the result. The difficulty has been strangely exaggerated and misapprehended. I can choose my current, and should I find *all* currents against me, I can make very tolerable headway with the propeller. We have had no incidents worth recording. The night promises fair.

P.S. [By Mr. Ainsworth.] I have little to record, except the fact (to me quite a surprising one) that, at an elevation equal to that of Cotopaxi, I experienced neither very intense cold, nor headache, nor difficulty of breathing; neither, I find, did Mr. Mason, nor Mr. Holland, nor Sir Everard. Mr. Osborne complained of constriction of the chest—but this soon wore off. We have flown at a great rate during the day, and we must be more than half way across the Atlantic. We have passed over some twenty or thirty vessels of various kinds, and all seem to be delightfully astonished. Crossing the ocean in a balloon is not so difficult a feat after all. *Omne ignotum pro magnifico. Mem.:* at 25,000 feet elevation the sky appears nearly black, and the stars are distinctly visible; while the sea does not seem convex (as one might suppose) but absolutely and most unequivocally *concave*.

"*Monday, the 8th.* [Mr. Mason's MS.] This morning we had again some little trouble with the rod of the propeller, which must be entirely remodelled, for fear of serious accident—I mean the steel rod, not the vanes. The latter could not be improved. The wind has been blowing steadily and strongly from the northeast all day; and so far fortune seems bent upon favoring us. Just before day, we were all somewhat alarmed at some odd noises and concussions in the balloon, accompanied with the apparent rapid subsidence of the whole machine. These phenomena were occasioned by the expansion of the gas, through increase of heat in the atmosphere, and the consequent disruption of the minute particles of ice with which the network had become encrusted during the night. Threw down several bottles to the vessels below. Saw one of them picked up by a large ship—seemingly one of the New York line packets. Endeavored to make out her name, but could not be sure of it. Mr. Osborne's telescope made it out something like 'Atalanta.' It is now twelve at night, and we are still going nearly west, at a rapid pace. The sea is peculiarly phosphorescent.

"P.S. [By Mr. Ainsworth.] It is now two A.M., and nearly calm, as well as I can judge—but it is very difficult to determine this point, since we move *with* the air so completely. I have not slept since quitting Wheal-Vor, but can stand it no longer, and must take a nap. We cannot be far from the American coast.

"*Tuesday, the 9th.* [Mr. Ainsworth's MS.] *One,* P.M. *We are in full view of the low coast of South Carolina.* The great problem is accomplished. We have crossed the

Atlantic—fairly and *easily* crossed it in a balloon! God be praised! Who shall say that any thing is impossible hereafter?"

The Journal here ceases. Some particulars of the descent were communicated, however, by Mr. Ainsworth to Mr. Forsyth. It was nearly dead calm when the voyagers first came in view of the coast, which was immediately recognized by both the seamen, and by Mr. Osborne. The latter gentleman having acquaintances at Fort Moultrie, it was immediately resolved to descend in its vicinity. The balloon was brought over the beach (the tide being out and the sand hard, smooth, and admirably adapted for a descent), and the grapnel let go, which took firm hold at once. The inhabitants of the island, and of the fort, thronged out, of course, to see the balloon; but it was with the greatest difficulty that any one could be made to credit the actual voyage—*the crossing of the Atlantic*. The grapnel caught at two P.M. precisely; and thus the whole voyage was completed in seventy-five hours; or rather less, counting from shore to shore. No serious accident occurred. No real danger was at any time apprehended. The balloon was exhausted and secured without trouble; and when the MS. from which this narrative is compiled was despatched from Charleston, the party were still at Fort Moultrie. Their further intentions were not ascertained; but we can safely promise our readers some additional information either on Monday or in the course of the next day, at furthest.

This is unquestionably the most stupendous, the most interesting, and the most important undertaking ever accomplished or even attempted by man. What magnificent events may ensue, it would be useless now to think of determining.

The Spectacles

MANY years ago, it was the fashion to ridicule the idea of "love at first sight"; but those who think, not less than those who feel deeply, have always advocated its existence. Modern discoveries, indeed, in what may be termed ethical magnetism or magnetæsthetics, render it probable that the most natural, and, consequently, the truest and most intense of the human affections are those which arise in the heart as if by electric sympathy—in a word, that the brightest and most enduring of the psychal fetters are those which are riveted by a glance. The confession I am about to make will add another to the already almost innumerable instances of the truth of the position.

My story requires that I should be somewhat minute. I am still a very young man—not yet twenty-two years of age. My name, at present, is a very usual and rather plebeian one—Simpson. I say "at present"; for it is only lately that I have been so called—having legislatively adopted this surname within the last year in order to receive a large inheritance left me by a distant male relative, Adolphus Simpson, Esq. The bequest was conditioned upon my taking the name of the testator—the family, not the Christian name; my Christian name is Napoleon Buonaparte—or, more properly, these are my first and middle appellations.

I assumed the name, Simpson, with some reluctance, as in my true patronym, Froissart, I felt a very pardonable pride—believing that I could trace a descent from the immortal author of the "Chronicles." While on the subject of names, by the bye, I may mention a singular coincidence of sound attending the names of some of my immediate predecessors. My father was a Monsieur Froissart, of Paris. His wife—my mother, whom he married at fifteen—was a Mademoiselle Croissart, eldest daughter of Croissart the banker; whose wife, again, being only sixteen when married, was the eldest daughter of one Victor Voissart. Monsieur Voissart, very singularly, had married a lady of similar name—a Mademoiselle Moissart. She, too, was quite a child when married; and her mother, also, Madame Moissart, was only fourteen when led to the altar. These early marriages are usual in France. Here, however, are Moissart, Voissart, Croissart, and Froissart, all in the direct line of descent. My own name, though, as I say, became Simpson, by act of Legislature, and with so much repugnance on my part, that, at one period, I actually hesitated about accepting the legacy with the useless and annoying *proviso* attached.

As to personal endowments, I am by no means deficient. On the contrary, I believe that I am well made, and possess what nine tenths of the world would call a handsome face. In height I am five feet eleven. My hair is black and curling. My nose is sufficiently good. My eyes are large and gray; and although, in fact, they are weak to a very inconvenient degree, still no defect in this regard would be suspected from their appearance. The weakness itself, however, has always much annoyed me, and I have resorted to every remedy—short of wearing glasses. Being youthful and good-looking, I naturally dislike these, and have resolutely refused to employ them. I know nothing, indeed, which so disfigures the countenance of a young person, or so impresses every feature with an air of demureness, if not altogether of sanctimoniousness and of age. An eye-glass, on the other hand, has a savor of downright foppery and affectation. I have hitherto managed as well as I could without either. But something too much of these merely personal details, which, after all, are of little importance. I will content myself with saying, in addition, that my temperament is sanguine, rash, ardent, enthusiastic—and that all my life I have been a devoted admirer of the women.

One night last winter I entered a box at the P——Theatre, in company with a friend, Mr. Talbot. It was an opera night, and the bills presented a very rare attraction, so that the house was excessively crowded. We were in time, however,

to obtain the front seats which had been reserved for us, and into which, with some little difficulty, we elbowed our way.

For two hours my companion, who was a musical *fanatico*, gave his undivided attention to the stage; and, in the meantime, I amused myself by observing the audience, which consisted, in chief part, of the very *élite* of the city. Having satisfied myself upon this point, I was about turning my eyes to the *prima donna*, when they were arrested and riveted by a figure in one of the private boxes which had escaped my observation.

If I live a thousand years I can never forget the intense emotion with which I regarded this figure. It was that of a female, the most exquisite I had ever beheld. The face was so far turned toward the stage that, for some minutes, I could not obtain a view of it,—but the form was *divine*; no other word can sufficiently express its magnificent proportion,—and even the term "divine" seems ridiculously feeble as I write it.

The magic of a lovely form in woman—the necromancy of female gracefulness—was always a power which I had found it impossible to resist; but here was grace personified, incarnate, the *beau idéal* of my wildest and most enthusiastic visions. The figure, almost all of which the construction of the box permitted to be seen, was somewhat above the medium height, and nearly approached, without positively reaching, the majestic. Its perfect fullness and *tournure* were delicious. The head, of which only the back was visible, rivalled in outline that of the Greek Psyche, and was rather displayed than concealed by an elegant cap of *gaze aérienne*, which put me in mind of the *ventum textilem* of Apuleius. The right arm hung over the balustrade of the box, and thrilled every nerve of my frame with its exquisite symmetry. Its upper portion was drapeiried by one of the loose open sleeves now in fashion. This extended but little below the elbow. Beneath it was worn an under one of some frail material, close-fitting, and terminated by a cuff of rich lace, which fell gracefully over the top of the hand, revealing only the delicate fingers, upon one of which sparkled a diamond ring, which I at once saw was of extraordinary value. The admirable roundness of the wrist was well set off by a bracelet which encircled it, and which also was ornamented and clasped by a magnificent *aigrette* of jewels,—telling, in words that could not be mistaken, at once of the wealth and fastidious taste of the wearer.

I gazed at this queenly apparition for at least half an hour, as if I had been suddenly converted to stone; and, during this period, I felt the full force and truth of all that has been said or sung concerning "love at first sight." My feelings were totally different from any which I had hitherto experienced, in the presence of even the most celebrated specimens of female loveliness. An unaccountable,

and what I am compelled to consider a *magnetic*, sympathy of soul for soul, seemed to rivet, not only my vision, but my whole powers of thought and feeling, upon the admirable object before me. I saw—I felt—I knew that I was deeply, madly, irrevocably in love—and this even before seeing the face of the person beloved. So intense, indeed, was the passion that consumed me, that I really believe it would have received little if any abatement had the features, yet unseen, proved of merely ordinary character; so anomalous is the nature of the only true love—of the love at first sight—and so little really dependent is it upon the external conditions which only seem to create and control it.

While I was thus wrapped in admiration of this lovely vision, a sudden disturbance among the audience caused her to turn her head partially toward me, so that I beheld the entire profile of the face. Its beauty even exceeded my anticipations—and yet there was something about it which disappointed me without my being able to tell exactly what it was. I said "disappointed," but this is not altogether the word. My sentiments were at once quieted and exalted. They partook less of transport and more of calm enthusiasm—of enthusiastic repose. This state of feeling arose, perhaps, from the Madonna-like and matronly air of the face; and yet I at once understood that it could not have arisen entirely from this. There was something else—some mystery which I could not develop—some expression about the countenance which slightly disturbed me while it greatly heightened my interest. In fact, I was just in that condition of mind which prepares a young and susceptible man for any act of extravagance. Had the lady been alone, I should undoubtedly have entered her box and accosted her at all hazards; but, fortunately, she was attended by two companions—a gentleman, and a strikingly beautiful woman, to all appearance a few years younger than herself.

I revolved in my mind a thousand schemes by which I might obtain, hereafter, an introduction to the elder lady, or, for the present, at all events, a more distinct view of her beauty. I would have removed my position to one nearer her own, but the crowded state of the theatre rendered this impossible; and the stern decrees of Fashion had, of late, imperatively prohibited the use of the opera-glass, in a case such as this, even had I been so fortunate as to have one with me—but I had not—and was thus in despair.

At length I bethought me of applying to my companion.

"Talbot," I said, "*you* have an opera-glass. Let me have it."

"An opera-glass!—no!—what do you suppose *I* would be doing with an opera-glass?" Here he turned impatiently toward the stage.

"But, Talbot," I continued, pulling him by the shoulder, "listen to me, will you? Do you see the stage-box?—there!—no, the next.—Did you ever behold as lovely a woman?"

"She is very beautiful, no doubt," he said.

"I wonder who she can be?"

"Why, in the name of all that is angelic, don't you *know* who she is? 'Not to know her argues yourself unknown.' She is the celebrated Madame Lalande—the beauty of the day *par excellence*, and the talk of the whole town. Immensely wealthy too—a widow—and a great match—has just arrived from Paris."

"Do you know her?"

"Yes—I have the honor."

"Will you introduce me?"

"Assuredly—with the greatest pleasure; when shall it be?"

"To-morrow, at one, I will call upon you at B——'s."

"Very good; and now *do* hold your tongue, *if* you can."

In this latter respect I was forced to take Talbot's advice; for he remained obstinately deaf to every further question or suggestion, and occupied himself exclusively for the rest of the evening with what was transacting upon the stage.

In the meantime I kept my eyes riveted on Madame Lalande, and at length had the good fortune to obtain a full front view of her face. It was exquisitely lovely: this, of course, my heart had told me before, even had not Talbot fully satisfied me upon the point—but still the unintelligible something disturbed me. I finally concluded that my senses were impressed by a certain air of gravity, sadness, or, still more properly, of weariness, which took something from the youth and freshness of the countenance, only to endow it with a seraphic tenderness and majesty, and thus, of course, to my enthusiastic and romantic temperament, with an interest tenfold.

While I thus feasted my eyes, I perceived, at last, to my great trepidation, by an almost imperceptible start on the part of the lady, that she had become suddenly aware of the intensity of my gaze. Still, I was absolutely fascinated, and could not withdraw it, even for an instant. She turned aside her face, and again I saw only the chiselled contour of the back portion of the head. After some minutes, as if urged by curiosity to see if I was still looking, she gradually brought her face again around and again encountered my burning gaze. Her large dark eyes fell instantly, and a deep blush mantled her cheek. But what was my astonishment at perceiving that she not only did not a second time avert her head, but that she actually took from her girdle a double eye-glass—elevated it—adjusted it—and then regarded me through it, intently and deliberately, for the space of several minutes.

Had a thunderbolt fallen at my feet I could not have been more thoroughly astounded—astounded *only*—not offended or disgusted in the slightest degree; although an action so bold in any other woman would have been likely to offend or disgust. But the whole thing was done with so much quietude—so much *nonchalance*—so much repose—with so evident an air of the highest breeding, in short—that nothing of mere effrontery was perceptible, and my sole sentiments were those of admiration and surprise.

I observed that, upon her first elevation of the glass, she had seemed satisfied with a momentary inspection of my person, and was withdrawing the instrument, when, as if struck by a second thought, she resumed it, and so continued to regard me with fixed attention for the space of several minutes—for five minutes, at the very least, I am sure.

This action, so remarkable in an American theatre, attracted very general observation, and gave rise to an indefinite movement, or *buzz*, among the audience, which for a moment filled me with confusion, but produced no visible effect upon the countenance of Madame Lalande.

Having satisfied her curiosity—if such it was—she dropped the glass, and quietly gave her attention again to the stage; her profile now being turned toward myself, as before. I continued to watch her unremittingly, although I was fully conscious of my rudeness in so doing. Presently I saw the head slowly and slightly change its position; and soon I became convinced that the lady, while pretending to look at the stage was, in fact, attentively regarding myself. It is needless to say what effect this conduct, on the part of so fascinating a woman, had upon my excitable mind.

Having thus scrutinized me for perhaps a quarter of an hour, the fair object of my passion addressed the gentleman who attended her, and, while she spoke, I saw distinctly, by the glances of both, that the conversation had reference to myself.

Upon its conclusion, Madame Lalande again turned toward the stage, and, for a few minutes, seemed absorbed in the performances. At the expiration of this period, however, I was thrown into an extremity of agitation by seeing her unfold, for the second time, the eye-glass which hung at her side, fully confront me as before, and, disregarding the renewed buzz of the audience, survey me, from head to foot, with the same miraculous composure which had previously so delighted and confounded my soul.

This extraordinary behavior, by throwing me into a perfect fever of excitement—into an absolute delirium of love—served rather to embolden than to disconcert me. In the mad intensity of my devotion, I forgot everything but the presence and the majestic loveliness of the vision which confronted my gaze. Watching my opportunity, when I thought the audience were fully engaged with the opera, I at length caught the eyes of Madame Lalande, and, upon the instant, made a slight but unmistakable bow.

She blushed very deeply—then averted her eyes—then slowly and cautiously looked around, apparently to see if my rash action had been noticed—then leaned over toward the gentleman who sat by her side.

I now felt a burning sense of the impropriety I had committed, and expected nothing less than instant exposure; while a vision of pistols upon the morrow floated rapidly and uncomfortably through my brain. I was greatly and immediately relieved, however, when I saw the lady merely hand the gentleman a play-bill, without speaking, but the reader may form some feeble conception of my astonishment—of my *profound* amazement—my delirious bewilderment of heart and soul—when, instantly afterward, having again glanced furtively around, she allowed her bright eyes to set fully and steadily upon my own, and then, with a faint smile, disclosing a bright line of her pearly teeth, made two distinct, pointed, and unequivocal affirmative inclinations of the head.

It is useless, of course, to dwell upon my joy—upon my transport—upon my illimitable ecstasy of heart. If ever man was mad with excess of happiness, it was myself at that moment. I loved. This was my *first* love—so I felt it to be. It was love supreme—indescribable. It was "love at first sight;" and at first sight, too, it had been appreciated and *returned*.

Yes, returned. How and why should I doubt it for an instant. What other construction could I possibly put upon such conduct, on the part of a lady so beautiful—so wealthy—evidently so accomplished—of so high breeding—of so lofty a position in society—in every regard so entirely respectable as I felt assured was Madame Lalande? Yes, she loved me—she returned the enthusiasm of my love, with an enthusiasm as blind—as uncompromising—as uncalculating—as abandoned—and as utterly unbounded as my own! These delicious fancies and reflections, however, were now interrupted by the falling of the drop-curtain. The audience arose; and the usual tumult immediately supervened. Quitting Talbot abruptly, I made every effort to force my way into closer proximity with Madame Lalande. Having failed in this, on account of the crowd, I at length gave up the chase, and bent my steps homeward; consoling myself for my disappointment in not having been able to touch even the hem of her robe, by the reflection that I should be introduced by Talbot, in due form, upon the morrow.

This morrow at last came; that is to say, a day finally dawned upon a long and weary night of impatience; and then the hours until "one" were snail-paced, dreary, and innumerable. But even Stamboul, it is said, shall have an end, and there came an end to this long delay. The clock struck. As the last echo ceased, I stepped into B——'s and inquired for Talbot.

"Out," said the footman—Talbot's own.

"Out!" I replied, staggering back half a dozen paces—"let me tell you, my fine fellow, that this thing is thoroughly impossible and impracticable; Mr. Talbot is *not* out. What do you mean?"

"Nothing, sir; only Mr. Talbot is not in. That's all. He rode over to S——, immediately after breakfast, and left word that he would not be in town again for a week."

I stood petrified with horror and rage. I endeavored to reply, but my tongue refused its office. At length I turned on my heel, livid with wrath, and inwardly consigning the whole tribe of the Talbots to the innermost regions of Erebus. It was evident that my considerate friend, *il fanatico*, had quite forgotten his appointment with myself—had forgotten it as soon as it was made. At no time was he a very scrupulous man of his word. There was no help for it; so smothering my vexation as well as I could, I strolled moodily up the street, propounding futile inquiries about Madame Lalande to every male acquaintance I met. By report she was known, I found, to all—to many by sight—but she had been in town only a few weeks, and there were very few, therefore, who claimed her personal acquaintance. These few, being still comparatively strangers, could not, or would not, take the liberty of introducing me through the formality of a morning call. While I stood thus, in despair, conversing with a trio of friends upon the all-absorbing subject of my heart, it so happened that the subject itself passed by.

"As I live, there she is!" cried one.

"Surprisingly beautiful!" exclaimed a second.

"An angel upon earth!" ejaculated a third.

I looked; and in an open carriage which approached us, passing slowly down the street, sat the enchanting vision of the opera, accompanied by the younger lady who had occupied a portion of her box.

"Her companion also wears remarkably well," said the one of my trio who had spoken first.

"Astonishingly," said the second; "still quite a brilliant air, but art will do wonders. Upon my word, she looks better than she did at Paris five years ago. A beautiful woman still;—don't you think so, Froissart?—Simpson, I mean."

"*Still!*" said I, "and why shouldn't she be? But compared with her friend she is as a rushlight to the evening star—a glow-worm to Antares."

"Ha! ha! ha!—why, Simpson, you have an astonishing tact at making discoveries—original ones, I mean." And here we separated, while one of the trio began humming a gay *vaudeville*, of which I caught only the lines—

Ninon, Ninon, Ninon à bas—

À bas Ninon De L'Enclos!

During this little scene, however, one thing had served greatly to console me, although it fed the passion by which I was consumed. As the carriage of Madame Lalande rolled by our group, I had observed that she recognized me; and more than this, she had blessed me, by the most seraphic of all imaginable smiles, with no equivocal mark of the recognition.

As for an introduction, I was obliged to abandon all hope of it, until such time as Talbot should think proper to return from the country. In the meantime I perseveringly frequented every reputable place of public amusement; and, at length, at the theatre, where I first saw her, I had the supreme bliss of meeting her, and of exchanging glances with her once again. This did not occur, however, until the lapse of a fortnight. Every day, in the *interim*, I had inquired for Talbot at his hotel, and every day had been thrown into a spasm of wrath by the everlasting "Not come home yet" of his footman.

Upon the evening in question, therefore, I was in a condition little short of madness. Madame Lalande, I had been told, was a Parisian—had lately arrived from Paris—might she not suddenly return?—return before Talbot came back—and might she not be thus lost to me forever? The thought was too terrible to bear. Since my future happiness was at issue, I resolved to act with a manly decision. In a word, upon the breaking up of the play, I traced the lady to her residence, noted the address, and the next morning sent her a full and elaborate letter, in which I poured out my whole heart.

I spoke boldly, freely—in a word, I spoke with passion. I concealed nothing—nothing even of my weakness. I alluded to the romantic circumstances of our first meeting—even to the glances which had passed between us. I went so far as to say that I felt assured of her love; while I offered this assurance, and my own intensity of devotion, as two excuses for my otherwise unpardonable conduct. As a third, I spoke of my fear that she might quit the city before I could have the opportunity of a formal introduction. I concluded the most wildly enthusiastic epistle ever penned, with a frank declaration of my worldly circumstances—of my affluence—and with an offer of my heart and of my hand.

In an agony of expectation I awaited the reply. After what seemed the lapse of a century it came.

Yes, *actually came*. Romantic as all this may appear, I really received a letter from Madame Lalande—the beautiful, the wealthy, the idolized Madame Lalande. Her eyes—her magnificent eyes, had not belied her noble heart. Like a true Frenchwoman, as she was, she had obeyed the frank dictates of her reason—the generous impulses of her nature—despising the conventional pruderies of the world. She had *not* scorned my proposals. She had *not* sheltered herself in silence. She had *not* returned my letter unopened. She had even sent me, in reply, one penned by her own exquisite fingers. It ran thus:

"Monsieur Simpson vill pardonne me for not compose de butefulle tong of his contrée so vell as might. It is only de late dat I am arrive, and not yet ave do opportunité for to—l'étudier.

"Vid dis apologie for the manière, I vill now say dat, hélas!—Monsieur Simpson ave guess but de too true. Need I say de more? Hélas! am I not ready speak de too moshe?

"EUGÉNIE LALAND."

This noble-spirited note I kissed a million times, and committed, no doubt, on its account, a thousand other extravagances that have now escaped my memory. Still Talbot *would* not return. Alas! could he have formed even the vaguest idea of the suffering his absence had occasioned his friend, would not his sympathizing nature have flown immediately to my relief? Still, however, he came

not. I wrote. He replied. He was detained by urgent business—but would shortly

return. He begged me not to be impatient—to moderate my transports—to read

soothing books—to drink nothing stronger than Hock—and to bring the conso-

lations of philosophy to my aid. The fool! if he could not come himself, why, in

the name of every thing rational, could he not have enclosed me a letter of pres-

entation? I wrote him again, entreating him to forward one forthwith. My letter

was returned by *that* footman, with the following endorsement in pencil. The

scoundrel had joined his master in the country:

"Left S——yesterday, for parts unknown—did not say where—or when be back—so thought

best to return letter, knowing your handwriting, and as how you is always, more or less, in a hurry.

"Yours sincerely, STUBBS."

After this, it is needless to say, that I devoted to the infernal deities both

master and valet:—but there was little use in anger, and no consolation at all in

complaint.

But I had yet a resource left, in my constitutional audacity. Hitherto it

had served me well, and I now resolved to make it avail me to the end. Besides, after the correspondence which had passed between us, what act of mere informality *could* I commit, within bounds, that ought to be regarded as indecorous by Madame Lalande? Since the affair of the letter, I had been in the habit of watching her house, and thus discovered that, about twilight, it was her custom to promenade, attended only by a negro in livery, in a public square overlooked by her windows. Here, amid the luxuriant and shadowing groves, in the gray gloom of a sweet midsummer evening, I observed my opportunity and accosted her.

The better to deceive the servant in attendance, I did this with the assured air of an old and familiar acquaintance. With a presence of mind truly Parisian, she took the cue at once, and, to greet me, held out the most bewitchingly little of hands. The valet at once fell into the rear; and now, with hearts full to overflowing, we discoursed long and unreservedly of our love.

As Madame Lalande spoke English even less fluently than she wrote it, our conversation was necessarily in French. In this sweet tongue, so adapted to passion, I gave loose to the impetuous enthusiasm of my nature, and, with all the eloquence I could command, besought her to consent to an immediate marriage.

At this impatience she smiled. She urged the old story of decorum—that bug-bear which deters so many from bliss until the opportunity for bliss has forever gone by. I had most imprudently made it known among my friends, she observed, that I desired her acquaintance—thus that I did not possess it—thus, again, there was no possibility of concealing the date of our first knowledge of each other. And then she adverted, with a blush, to the extreme recency of this date. To wed immediately would be improper—would be indecorous—would be *outré.* All this she said with a charming air of *naïveté* which enraptured while it grieved and convinced me. She went even so far as to accuse me, laughingly, of rashness—of imprudence. She bade me remember that I really even knew not who she was—what were her prospects, her connections, her standing in society. She begged me, but with a sigh, to reconsider my proposal, and termed my love an infatuation—a will o' the wisp—a fancy or fantasy of the moment—a baseless and unstable creation rather of the imagination than of the heart. These things she uttered as the shadows of the sweet twilight gathered darkly and more darkly around us—and then, with a gentle pressure of her fairy-like hand, overthrew, in a single sweet instant, all the argumentative fabric she had reared.

I replied as best I could—as only a true lover can. I spoke at length, and perseveringly of my devotion, of my passion—of her exceeding beauty, and of my own enthusiastic admiration. In conclusion, I dwelt, with a convincing energy, upon the perils that encompass the course of love—that course of true love that never did run smooth,—and thus deduced the manifest danger of rendering that course unnecessarily long.

This latter argument seemed finally to soften the rigor of her determination. She relented; but there was yet an obstacle, she said, which she felt assured I had not properly considered. This was a delicate point—for a woman to urge, especially so; in mentioning it, she saw that she must make a sacrifice of her feelings; still, for *me*, every sacrifice should be made. She alluded to the topic of *age*. Was I aware—was I fully aware of the discrepancy between us? That the age of the husband, should surpass by a few years—even by fifteen or twenty—the age of the wife, was regarded by the world as admissible, and, indeed, as even proper; but she had always entertained the belief that the years of the wife should *never* exceed in number those of the husband. A discrepancy of this unnatural kind gave rise, too frequently, alas! to a life of unhappiness. Now she was aware that my own age did not exceed two and twenty; and I, on the contrary, perhaps, was *not* aware that the years of my Eugénie extended very considerably beyond that sum.

About all this there was a nobility of soul—a dignity of candor—which delighted—which enchanted me—which eternally riveted my chains. I could scarcely restrain the excessive transport which possessed me.

"My sweetest Eugénie," I cried, "what is all this about which you are discoursing? Your years surpass in some measure my own. But what then? The customs of the world are so many conventional follies. To those who love as ourselves, in what respect differs a year from an hour? I am twenty-two, you say; granted: indeed, you may as well call me, at once, twenty-three. Now you yourself, my dearest Eugénie, can have numbered no more than—can have numbered no more than—no more than—than—than—than—"

Here I paused for an instant, in the expectation that Madame Lalande would interrupt me by supplying her true age. But a Frenchwoman is seldom direct, and has always, by way of answer to an embarrassing query, some little practical reply of her own. In the present instance, Eugénie, who for a few moments past had seemed to be searching for something in her bosom, at length let fall upon the grass a miniature, which I immediately picked up and presented to her.

"Keep it!" she said, with one of her most ravishing smiles. "Keep it for my sake—for the sake of her whom it too flatteringly represents. Besides, upon the back of the trinket you may discover, perhaps, the very information you seem to desire. It is now, to be sure, growing rather dark—but you can examine it at your leisure in the morning. In the meantime, you shall be my escort home to-night. My friends are about holding a little musical *levée*. I can promise

you, too, some good singing. We French are not nearly so punctilious as you Americans, and I shall have no difficulty in smuggling you in, in the character of an old acquaintance."

With this, she took my arm, and I attended her home. The mansion was quite a fine one, and, I believe, furnished in good taste. Of this latter point, however, I am scarcely qualified to judge; for it was just dark as we arrived; and in American mansions of the better sort lights seldom, during the heat of summer, make their appearance at this, the most pleasant period of the day. In about an hour after my arrival, to be sure, a single shaded solar lamp was lit in the principal drawing-room; and this apartment, I could thus see, was arranged with unusual good taste and even splendor; but two other rooms of the suite, and in which the company chiefly assembled, remained, during the whole evening, in a very agreeable shadow. This is a well-conceived custom, giving the party at least a choice of light or shade, and one which our friends over the water could not do better than immediately adopt.

The evening thus spent was unquestionably the most delicious of my life. Madame Lalande had not overrated the musical abilities of her friends; and the singing I here heard I had never heard excelled in any private circle out of Vienna. The instrumental performers were many and of superior talents. The vocalists were chiefly ladies, and no individual sang less than well. At length, upon a peremptory call for "Madame Lalande," she arose at once, without affectation or demur, from the *chaise longue* upon which she had sat by my side, and, accompanied by one or two gentlemen and her female friend of the opera, repaired to the piano in the main drawing-room. I would have escorted her myself, but felt that, under the circumstances of my introduction to the house, I had better remain unobserved where I was. I was thus deprived of the pleasure of seeing, although not of hearing, her sing.

The impression she produced upon the company seemed electrical—but the effect upon myself was something even more. I know not how adequately to describe it. It arose in part, no doubt, from the sentiment of love with which I was imbued; but chiefly from my conviction of the extreme sensibility of the singer. It is beyond the reach of art to endow either air or recitative with more impassioned *expression* than was hers. Her utterance of the romance in Otello— the tone with which she gave the words "*Sul mio sasso,*" in the Capuletti—is ringing in my memory yet. Her lower tones were absolutely miraculous. Her voice embraced three complete octaves, extending from the contralto D to the D upper soprano, and, though sufficiently powerful to have filled the San Carlos, executed, with the minutest precision, every difficulty of vocal composition—

ascending and descending scales, cadences, or *fiorituri*. In the finale of the Son-
nambula, she brought about a most remarkable effect at the words:

Ah! non guinge uman pensiero
Al contento ond 'io son piena.

Here, in imitation of Malibran, she modified the original phrase of Bellini,
so as to let her voice descend to the tenor G, when, by a rapid transition, she
struck the G above the treble stave, springing over an interval of two octaves.

Upon rising from the piano after these miracles of vocal execution, she
resumed her seat by my side; when I expressed to her, in terms of the deepest
enthusiasm, my delight at her performance. Of my surprise I said nothing,
and yet was I most unfeignedly surprised; for a certain feebleness, or rather a
certain tremulous indecision of voice in ordinary conversation, had prepared
me to anticipate that, in singing, she would not acquit herself with any remarkable ability.

Our conversation was now long, earnest, uninterrupted, and totally unre-
served. She made me relate many of the earlier passages of my life, and listened
with breathless attention to every word of the narrative. I concealed nothing—
felt that I had a right to conceal nothing—from her confiding affection.

Encouraged by her candor upon the delicate point of her age, I entered, with perfect frankness, not only into a detail of my many minor vices, but made full confession of those moral and even of those physical infirmities, the disclosure of which, in demanding so much higher a degree of courage, is so much surer an evidence of love. I touched upon my college indiscretions—upon my extravagances—upon my carousals—upon my debts—upon my flirtations. I even went so far as to speak of a slightly hectic cough with which, at one time, I had been troubled—of a chronic rheumatism—of a twinge of hereditary gout—and, in conclusion, of the disagreeable and inconvenient, but hitherto carefully concealed, weakness of my eyes.

"Upon this latter point," said Madame Lalande, laughingly, "you have been surely injudicious in coming to confession; for, without the confession, I take it for granted that no one would have accused you of the crime. By the by," she continued, "have you any recollection—" and here I fancied that a blush, even through the gloom of the apartment, became distinctly visible upon her cheek— "have you any recollection, *mon cher ami*, of this little ocular assistant which now depends from my neck?"

As she spoke she twirled in her fingers the identical double eye-glass, which had so overwhelmed me with confusion at the opera.

"Full well—alas! do I remember it," I exclaimed, pressing passionately the delicate hand which offered the glasses for my inspection. They formed a complex and magnificent toy, richly chased and filigreed, and gleaming with jewels which, even in the deficient light, I could not help perceiving were of high value.

"*Eh bien! mon ami*," she resumed with a certain *empressment* of manner that rather surprised me—"*Eh bien! mon ami*, you have earnestly besought of me a favor which you have been pleased to denominate priceless. You have demanded of me my hand upon the morrow. Should I yield to your entreaties—and, I may add, to the pleadings of my own bosom—would I not be entitled to demand of you a very—a very little boon in return?"

"Name it!" I exclaimed with an energy that had nearly drawn upon us the observation of the company, and restrained by their presence alone from throwing myself impetuously at her feet. "Name it, my beloved, my Eugénie, my own!—name it!—but, alas! it is already yielded ere named."

"You shall conquer, then, *mon ami*," said she, "for the sake of the Eugénie whom you love, this little weakness which you have at last confessed—this weakness more moral than physical—and which, let me assure you, is so unbecoming the nobility of your real nature—so inconsistent with the candor of your usual character—and which, if permitted further control, will assuredly involve you, sooner or later, in some very disagreeable scrape. You shall conquer, for my sake, this affectation which leads you, as you yourself acknowledge, to the tacit or implied denial of your infirmity of vision. For, this infirmity you virtually deny, in refusing to employ the customary means for its relief. You will understand me to say, then, that I wish you to wear spectacles:—ah, hush!—you have already consented to wear them, *for my sake*. You shall accept the little toy which I now hold in my hand, and which, though admirable as an aid to vision, is really of no very immense value as a gem. You perceive that, by a trifling modification thus— or thus—it can be adapted to the eyes in the form of spectacles, or worn in the waistcoat pocket as an eye-glass. It is in the former mode, however, and habitu- ally, that you have already consented to wear it *for my sake*."

This request—must I confess it?—confused me in no little degree. But the condition with which it was coupled rendered hesitation, of course, a matter altogether out of the question.

"It is done!" I cried, with all the enthusiasm that I could muster at the moment. "It is done—it is most cheerfully agreed. I sacrifice every feeling for your sake. To-night I wear this dear eye-glass, *as* an eye-glass, and upon my heart; but with the earliest dawn of that morning which gives me the pleasure of call- ing you wife, I will place it upon my—upon my nose,—and there wear it ever afterward, in the less romantic, and less fashionable, but certainly in the more serviceable, form which you desire."

Our conversation now turned upon the details of our arrangements for the morrow. Talbot, I learned from my betrothed, had just arrived in town. I was to see him at once, and procure a carriage. The *soirée* would scarcely break up before two; and by this hour the vehicle was to be at the door; when, in the confusion occasioned by the departure of the company, Madame L. could easily enter it unobserved. We were then to call at the house of a clergyman who would be in waiting; there be married, drop Talbot, and proceed on a short tour to the East; leaving the fashionable world at home to make whatever comments upon the matter it thought best.

Having planned all this, I immediately took leave, and went in search of Talbot, but, on the way, I could not refrain from stepping into a hotel, for the purpose of inspecting the miniature; and this I did by the powerful aid of the glasses. The countenance was a surpassingly beautiful one! Those large luminous eyes!—that proud Grecian nose!—those dark luxuriant curls!—"Ah!" said I, exultingly to myself, "this is indeed the speaking image of my beloved!" I turned the reverse, and discovered the words—"Eugénie Lalande—aged twenty-seven years and seven months."

I found Talbot at home, and proceeded at once to acquaint him with my good fortune. He professed excessive astonishment, of course, but congratulated me most cordially, and proffered every assistance in his power. In a word, we carried out our arrangement to the letter; and, at two in the morning, just ten minutes after the ceremony, I found myself in a close carriage with Madame Lalande—with Mrs. Simpson, I should say—and driving at a great rate out of town, in a direction northeast by north, half-north.

It had been determined for us by Talbot, that, as we were to be up all night, we should make our first stop at C——, a village about twenty miles from the city, and there get an early breakfast and some repose, before proceeding upon our route. At four precisely, therefore, the carriage drew up at the door of the principal inn. I handed my adored wife out, and ordered breakfast forthwith. In the meantime we were shown into a small parlor, and sat down.

It was now nearly if not altogether daylight; and, as I gazed, enraptured, at the angel by my side, the singular idea came, all at once, into my head, that this was really the very first moment since my acquaintance with the celebrated loveliness of Madame Lalande, that I had enjoyed a near inspection of that loveliness by daylight at all.

"And now, *mon ami*," said she, taking my hand, and so interrupting this train of reflection, "and now, *mon cher ami*, since we are indissolubly one—since I have yielded to your passionate entreaties, and performed my portion of our agreement—I presume you have not forgotten that you also have a little favor to bestow—a little promise which it is your intention to keep. Ah! let me see! Let me remember! Yes; full easily do I call to mind the precise words of the dear promise you made to Eugénie last night. Listen! You spoke thus: 'It is done!—it is most cheerfully agreed! I sacrifice every feeling for your sake. To-night I wear this dear eye-glass *as* an eye-glass, and upon my heart; but with the earliest dawn of that morning which gives me the privilege of calling you wife, I will place it upon my—upon my nose,—and there wear it ever afterward, in the less romantic, and less fashionable, but certainly in the more serviceable, form which you desire.' These were the exact words, my beloved husband, were they not?"

"They were," I said; "you have an excellent memory; and assuredly, my beautiful Eugénie, there is no disposition on my part to evade the performance of the trivial promise they imply. See! Behold! they are becoming—rather—are they not?" And here, having arranged the glasses in the ordinary form of spectacles, I applied them gingerly in their proper position; while Madame Simpson, adjusting her cap, and folding her arms, sat bolt upright in her chair, in a somewhat stiff and prim, and indeed, in a somewhat undignified position.

"Goodness gracious me!" I exclaimed, almost at the very instant that the rim of the spectacles had settled upon my nose—"*My!* goodness gracious me!—why, what *can* be the matter with these glasses?" and taking them quickly off, I wiped them carefully with a silk handkerchief and adjusted them again.

But if, in the first instance, there had occurred something which occasioned me surprise, in the second this surprise became elevated into astonishment; and this astonishment was profound—was extreme—indeed I may say it was horrific. What, in the name of everything hideous, did this mean? Could I believe my eyes?—*could* I?—that was the question. Was that—was that—was that *rouge?* And were those—and were those—were those *wrinkles,* upon the visage of Eugénie Lalande? And oh! Jupiter, and every one of the gods and goddesses, little and big! what—what—what—*what* had become of her teeth? I dashed the spectacles violently to the ground, and, leaping to my feet, stood erect in the middle of the floor, confronting Mrs. Simpson, with my arms set a-kimbo, and grinning and foaming, but, at the same time, utterly speechless with terror and with rage.

Now I have already said that Madame Eugénie Lalande—that is to say, Simpson—spoke the English language but very little better than she wrote it; and for this reason she very properly never attempted to speak it upon ordinary occasions. But rage will carry a lady to any extreme; and in the present case it carried

Mrs. Simpson to the very extraordinary extreme of attempting to hold a conversation in a tongue that she did not altogether understand.

"Vell, Monsieur," said she, after surveying me, in great apparent astonishment, for some moments—"Vell, Monsieur?—and vat den?—vat de matter now? Is it de dance of de Saint Vitusse dat you ave? If not like me, vat for vy buy de pig in the poke?"

"You wretch!" said I, catching my breath—"you—you—you villainous old hag!"

"Ag?—ole?—me not so *ver* ole, after all! Me not one single day more dan de eighty-doo."

"Eighty-two!" I ejaculated, staggering to the wall—"eighty-two hundred thousand baboons! The miniature said twenty-seven years and seven months!"

"To be sure!—dat is so!—ver true! but den de portraite has been take for dese fifty-five year. Ven I go marry my segonde usbande, Monsieur Lalande, at dat time I had de portraite take for my daughter by my first usbande, Monsieur Moissart!"

"Moissart!" said I.

"Yes, Moissart," said she, mimicking my pronunciation, which, to speak the truth, was none of the best;—"and vat den? Vat *you* know about de Moissart?"

"Nothing, you old fright!—I know nothing about him at all; only I had an ancestor of that name, once upon a time."

"Dat name! and vat you ave for say to dat name? 'Tis ver *goot* name; and so is Voissart—dat is ver goot name too. My daughter, Mademoiselle Moissart, she marry von Monsieur Voissart,—and de name is bot *ver* respectaable name."

"Moissart?" I exclaimed, "and Voissart! Why, what is it you mean?"

"Vat I mean?—I mean Moissart and Voissart; and for de matter of dat, I mean Croissart and Froissart, too, if I only tink proper to mean it. My daughter's daughter, Mademoiselle Voissart, she marry von Monsieur Croissart, and den again, my daughter's grande daughter, Mademoiselle Croissart, she marry von Monsieur Froissart; and I suppose you say dat *dat* is not von *ver* respectaable name."

"Froissart!" said I, beginning to faint, "why surely you don't say Moissart, and Voissart, and Croissart, and Froissart?"

"Yes," she replied, leaning fully back in her chair, and stretching out her lower limbs at great length; "yes, Moissart, and Voissart, and Croissart, and Froissart. But Monsieur Froissart, he vas von *ver* big vat you call fool—he vas von ver great big donce like yourself—for he lef *la belle France* for come to dis stupide Amérique—and ven he get here he vent and ave von *ver* stupide, von *ver, ver* stupide sonn, so I hear, dough I not yet av ad de plaisir to meet vid him—neither me nor my companion, de Madame Stephanie Lalande. He is name de Napoleon Bonaparte Froissart, and I suppose you say dat *dat*, too, is not von *ver* respectable name."

Either the length or the nature of this speech, had the effect of working up Mrs. Simpson into a very extraordinary passion indeed; and as she made an end of it, with great labor, she jumped up from her chair like somebody bewitched, dropping upon the floor an entire universe of bustle as she jumped. Once upon her feet, she gnashed her gums, brandished her arms, rolled up her sleeves, shook her fist in my face, and concluded the performance by tearing the cap from her head, and with it an immense wig of the most valuable and beautiful black hair, the whole of which she dashed upon the ground with a yell, and there trampled and danced a fandango upon it, in an absolute ecstasy and agony of rage.

Meantime I sank aghast into the chair which she had vacated. "Moissart and Voissart!" I repeated, thoughtfully, as she cut one of her pigeon-wings, and "Croissart and Froissart!" as she completed another—"Moissart and Voissart and Croissart and Napoleon Bonaparte Froissart!—why, you ineffable old serpent, that's *me*—that's *me*—d'ye hear? that's *me*"—here I screamed at the top of my voice—"that's *me-e-e!* I am Napoleon Bonaparte Froissart! and if I haven't married my great, great, grandmother, I wish I may be everlastingly confounded!"

Madame Eugénie Lalande, *quasi* Simpson—formerly Moissart—was, in sober fact, my great, great, grandmother. In her youth she had been beautiful, and even at eighty-two, retained the majestic height, the sculptural contour of head, the fine eyes and the Grecian nose of her girlhood. By the aid of these, of pearl-powder, of rouge, of false hair, false teeth, and false *tournure*, as well as of the most skilful modistes of Paris, she contrived to hold a respectable footing among the beauties *en peu passées* of the French metropolis. In this respect, indeed, she might have been regarded as little less than the equal of the celebrated Ninon De L'Enclos.

She was immensely wealthy, and being left, for the second time, a widow without children, she bethought herself of my existence in America, and for the purpose of making me her heir, paid a visit to the United States, in company with a distant and exceedingly lovely relative of her second husband's—a Madame Stephanie Lalande.

At the opera, my great, great, grandmother's attention was arrested by my notice; and, upon surveying me through her eye-glass, she was struck with a certain family resemblance to herself. Thus interested, and knowing that the heir she sought was actually in the city, she made inquiries of her party respecting me. The gentleman who attended her knew my person, and told her who I was. The information thus obtained induced her to renew her scrutiny; and this scrutiny it was which so emboldened me that I behaved in the absurd manner already detailed. She returned my bow, however, under the impression that, by some odd accident, I had discovered her identity. When, deceived by my weakness of vision, and the arts of the toilet, in respect to the age and charms of the strange lady, I demanded so enthusiastically of Talbot who she was, he concluded that I meant the younger beauty, as a matter of course, and so informed me, with perfect truth, that she was "the celebrated widow, Madame Lalande."

In the street, next morning, my great, great, grandmother encountered Talbot, an old Parisian acquaintance; and the conversation, very naturally turned upon myself. My deficiencies of vision were then explained; for these were notorious, although I was entirely ignorant of their notoriety; and my good old relative discovered, much to her chagrin, that she had been deceived in supposing me aware of her identity, and that I had been merely making a fool of myself in making open love, in a theatre, to an old woman unknown. By way of punishing me for this imprudence, she concocted with Talbot a plot. He purposely kept out of my way to avoid giving me the introduction. My street inquiries about "the lovely widow, Madame Lalande," were supposed to refer to the younger lady, of course; and thus the conversation with the three gentlemen whom I encountered shortly after leaving Talbot's hotel will be easily explained, as also their allusion to Ninon De L'Enclos. I had no opportunity of seeing Madame Lalande closely during daylight, and, at her musical *soirée*, my silly weakness in refusing the aid of glasses effectually prevented me from making a discovery of her age. When "Madame Lalande" was called upon to sing, the younger lady was intended; and it was she who arose to obey the call; my great, great, grandmother, to further the deception, arising at the same moment and accompanying her to the piano in the main drawing-room. Had I decided upon escorting her thither, it had been her design to suggest the propriety of my remaining where I was; but my own prudential views rendered this unnecessary. The songs which I so much admired, and which so confirmed my impression of the youth of my mistress, were executed by Madame Stephanie Lalande. The eye-glass was presented by way of adding a reproof to the hoax—a sting to the epigram of the deception. Its presentation afforded an opportunity for the lecture upon affectation with which I was so especially edified. It is almost superfluous to add that the glasses of the instrument, as worn by the old lady, had been exchanged by her for a pair better adapted to my years. They suited me, in fact, to a T.

The clergyman, who merely pretended to tie the fatal knot, was a boon companion of Talbot's, and no priest. He was an excellent "whip," however; and having doffed his cassock to put on a great-coat, he drove the hack which conveyed the "happy couple" out of town. Talbot took a seat at his side. The two scoundrels were thus "in at the death," and through a half-open window of the back parlor of the inn, amused themselves in grinning at the *dénouement* of the drama. I believe I shall be forced to call them both out.

Nevertheless, I am *not* the husband of my great, great, grandmother; and this is a reflection which affords me infinite relief;—but I *am* the husband of Madame Lalande—of Madame Stephanie Lalande—with whom my good old relative, besides making me her sole heir when she dies—if she ever does—has been at the trouble of concocting me a match. In conclusion: I am done forever with *billets doux*, and am never to be met without SPECTACLES.

The System of Doctor Tarr
and Professor Fether

DURING the autumn of 18—, while on a tour through the extreme southern provinces of France, my route led me within a few miles of a certain *Maison de Santé* or private mad-house, about which I had heard much, in Paris, from my medical friends. As I had never visited a place of the kind, I thought the opportunity too good to be lost; and so proposed to my travelling companion (a gentleman with whom I had made casual acquaintance a few days before), that we should turn aside, for an hour or so, and look through the establishment. To this he objected—pleading haste, in the first place, and, in the second, a very usual horror at the sight of a lunatic. He begged of me, however, not to let any mere courtesy toward himself interfere with the gratification of my curiosity, and said that he would ride on leisurely, so that I might overtake him during the day, or, at all events, during the next. As he bade me good-bye, I bethought me that there might be some difficulty in obtaining access to the premises, and mentioned my fears on this point. He replied that, in fact, unless I had personal knowledge of the superintendent, Monsieur Maillard, or some credential in the way of a letter, a difficulty might be found to exist, as the regulations of these private mad-houses were more rigid than the public hospital laws. For himself, he added, he had, some years since, made the acquaintance of Maillard, and would so far assist me as to ride up to the door and introduce me; although his feelings on the subject of lunacy would not permit of his entering the house.

I thanked him, and, turning from the main road, we entered a grass-grown by-path, which, in half an hour, nearly lost itself in a dense forest, clothing the base of a mountain. Through this dank and gloomy wood we rode some two miles, when the *Maison de Santé* came in view. It was a fantastic *château*, much dilapidated, and indeed scarcely tenantable through age and neglect. Its aspect inspired me with absolute dread, and, checking my horse, I half resolved to turn back. I soon, however, grew ashamed of my weakness, and proceeded.

As we rode up to the gate-way, I perceived it slightly open, and the visage of a man peering through. In an instant afterward, this man came forth, accosted my companion by name, shook him cordially by the hand, and begged him to alight. It was Monsieur Maillard himself. He was a portly, fine-looking gentleman of the old school, with a polished manner, and a certain air of gravity, dignity, and authority which was very impressive.

My friend, having presented me, mentioned my desire to inspect the establishment, and received Monsieur Maillard's assurance that he would show me all attention, now took leave, and I saw him no more.

When he had gone, the superintendent ushered me into a small and exceedingly neat parlor, containing, among other indications of refined taste, many books, drawings, pots of flowers, and musical instruments. A cheerful fire blazed upon the hearth. At a piano, singing an aria from Bellini, sat a young and very beautiful woman, who, at my entrance, paused in her song, and received me with graceful courtesy. Her voice was low, and her whole manner subdued. I thought, too, that I perceived the traces of sorrow in her countenance, which was excessively, although to my taste, not unpleasingly, pale. She was attired in deep mourning, and excited in my bosom a feeling of mingled respect, interest, and admiration.

I had heard, at Paris, that the institution of Monsieur Maillard was managed upon what is vulgarly termed the "system of soothing"—that all punishments were avoided—that even confinement was seldom resorted to—that the

patients, while secretly watched, were left much apparent liberty, and that most of them were permitted to roam about the house and grounds in the ordinary apparel of persons in right mind.

Keeping these impressions in view, I was cautious in what I said before the young lady; for I could not be sure that she was sane; and, in fact, there was a certain restless brilliancy about her eyes which half led me to imagine she was not. I confined my remarks, therefore, to general topics, and to such as I thought would not be displeasing or exciting even to a lunatic. She replied in a perfectly rational manner to all that I said; and even her original observations were marked with the soundest good sense; but a long acquaintance with the metaphysics of *mania*, had taught me to put no faith in such evidence of sanity, and I continued to practise, throughout the interview, the caution with which I commenced it.

Presently a smart footman in livery brought in a tray with fruit, wine, and other refreshments, of which I partook, the lady soon afterward leaving the room. As she departed I turned my eyes in an inquiring manner toward my host.

"No," he said, "oh, no—a member of my family—my niece, and a most accomplished woman."

"I beg a thousand pardons for the suspicion," I replied, "but of course you will know how to excuse me. The excellent administration of your affairs here is well understood in Paris, and I thought it just possible, you know—"

"Yes, yes—say no more—or rather it is myself who should thank you for the commendable prudence you have displayed. We seldom find so much of forethought in young men; and, more than once, some unhappy *contre-temps* has occurred in consequence of thoughtlessness on the part of our visitors. While my former system was in operation, and my patients were permitted the privilege of roaming to and fro at will, they were often aroused to a dangerous frenzy by injudicious persons who called to inspect the house. Hence I was obliged to enforce a rigid system of exclusion; and none obtained access to the premises upon whose discretion I could not rely."

"While your *former* system was in operation!" I said, repeating his words— "do I understand you, then, to say that the 'soothing system' of which I have heard so much is no longer in force?"

"It is now," he replied, "several weeks since we have concluded to renounce it forever."

"Indeed! you astonish me!"

"We found it, sir," he said, with a sigh, "absolutely necessary to return to the old usages. The *danger* of the soothing system was, at all times, appalling; and its advantages have been much overrated. I believe, sir, that in this house it has been given a fair trial, if ever in any. We did every thing that rational humanity could suggest. I am sorry that you could not have paid us a visit at an earlier period, that you might have judged for yourself. But I presume you are conversant with the soothing practice—with its details."

"Not altogether. What I have heard has been at third or fourth hand."

"I may state the system, then, in general terms, as one in which the patients were *menagés*—humored. We contradicted *no* fancies which entered the brains of the mad. On the contrary, we not only indulged but encouraged them; and many of our most permanent cures have been thus effected. There is no argument which so touches the feeble reason of the madman as the *reductio ad absurdum*. We have had men, for example, who fancied themselves chickens. The cure was, to insist upon the thing as a fact—to accuse the patient of stupidity in not sufficiently perceiving it to be a fact—and thus to refuse him any other diet for a week than that which properly appertains to a chicken. In this manner a little corn and gravel were made to perform wonders."

"But was this species of acquiescence all?"

"By no means. We put much faith in amusements of a simple kind, such as music, dancing, gymnastic exercises generally, cards, certain classes of books, and so forth. We affected to treat each individual as if for some ordinary physical disorder; and the word 'lunacy' was never employed. A great point was to set each lunatic to guard the actions of all the others. To repose confidence in the understanding or discretion of a madman, is to gain him body and soul. In this way we were enabled to dispense with an expensive body of keepers."

"And you had no punishments of any kind?"

"None."

"And you never confined your patients?"

"Very rarely. Now and then, the malady of some individual growing to a crisis, or taking a sudden turn of fury, we conveyed him to a secret cell, lest his disorder should infect the rest, and there kept him until we could dismiss him to his friends—for with the raging maniac we have nothing to do. He is usually removed to the public hospitals."

"And you have now changed all this—and you think for the better?"

"Decidedly. The system had its disadvantages, and even its dangers. It is now, happily, exploded throughout all the *Maisons de Santé* of France."

"I am very much surprised," I said, "at what you tell me; for I made sure that, at this moment, no other method of treatment for mania existed in any portion of the country."

"You are young yet, my friend," replied my host, "but the time will arrive when you will learn to judge for yourself of what is going on in the world, without trusting to the gossip of others. Believe nothing you hear, and only one-half that you see. Now about our *Maisons de Santé*, it is clear that some ignoramus has misled you. After dinner, however, when you have sufficiently recovered from the fatigue of your ride, I will be happy to take you over the house, and introduce to you a system which, in my opinion, and in that of every one who has witnessed its operation, is incomparably the most effectual as yet devised."

"Your own?" I inquired—"one of your own invention?"

"I am proud," he replied, "to acknowledge that it is—at least in some measure."

In this manner I conversed with Monsieur Maillard for an hour or two, during which he showed me the gardens and conservatories of the place.

"I cannot let you see my patients," he said, "just at present. To a sensitive mind there is always more or less of the shocking in such exhibitions; and I do not wish to spoil your appetite for dinner. We will dine. I can give you some veal *à la Menehoult*, with cauliflowers in *velouté* sauce—after that a glass of *Clos de Vougeôt*—then your nerves will be sufficiently steadied."

At six, dinner was announced; and my host conducted me into a large *salle à manger*, where a very numerous company were assembled—twenty-five or thirty

in all. They were, apparently, people of rank—certainly of high breeding—

although their habiliments, I thought, were extravagantly rich, partaking some-

what too much of the ostentatious finery of the *vielle cour*. I noticed that at least

two thirds of these guests were ladies; and some of the latter were by no means

accoutred in what a Parisian would consider good taste at the present day. Many

females, for example, whose age could not have been less than seventy were

bedecked with a profusion of jewelry, such as rings, bracelets, and ear-rings, and

wore their bosoms and arms shamefully bare. I observed, too, that very few of the

dresses were well made—or, at least, that very few of them fitted the wearers. In

looking about, I discovered the interesting girl to whom Monsieur Maillard had

presented me in the little parlor; but my surprise was great to see her wearing a

hoop and farthingale, with high-heeled shoes, and a dirty cap of Brussels lace, so

much too large for her that it gave her face a ridiculously diminutive expression.

When I had first seen her, she was attired, most becomingly, in deep mourning.

There was an air of oddity, in short, about the dress of the whole party, which, at

first, caused me to recur to my original idea of the "soothing system," and to fancy

that Monsieur Maillard had been willing to deceive me until after dinner, that I

might experience no uncomfortable feelings during the repast, at finding myself

dining with lunatics; but I remembered having been informed, in Paris, that the southern provincialists were a peculiarly eccentric people, with a vast number of antiquated notions; and then, too, upon conversing with several members of the company, my apprehensions were immediately and fully dispelled.

The dining-room itself, although perhaps sufficiently comfortable and of good dimensions, had nothing too much of elegance about it. For example, the floor was uncarpeted; in France, however, a carpet is frequently dispensed with. The windows, too, were without curtains; the shutters, being shut, were securely fastened with iron bars, applied diagonally, after the fashion of our ordinary shop-shutters. The apartment, I observed, formed, in itself, a wing of the *château*, and thus the windows were on three sides of the parallelogram, the door being at the other. There were no less than ten windows in all.

The table was superbly set out. It was loaded with plate, and more than loaded with delicacies. The profusion was absolutely barbaric. There were meats enough to have feasted the Anakim. Never, in all my life, had I witnessed so lavish, so wasteful an expenditure of the good things of life. There seemed very little taste, however, in the arrangements; and my eyes, accustomed to quiet lights, were sadly offended by the prodigious glare of a multitude of wax candles, which, in silver *candelabra*, were deposited upon the table, and all about the room, wherever it was possible to find a place. There were several active servants in attendance; and, upon a large table, at the farther end of the apartment, were seated seven or eight people with fiddles, fifes, trombones, and a drum. These fellows annoyed me very much, at intervals, during the repast, by an infinite variety of noises, which were intended for music, and which appeared to afford much entertainment to all present, with the exception of myself.

Upon the whole, I could not help thinking that there was much of the *bizarre* about every thing I saw—but then the world is made up of all kinds of persons, with all modes of thought, and all sorts of conventional customs. I had travelled, too, so much, as to be quite an adept at the *nil admirari*; so I took my seat very coolly at the right hand of my host, and, having an excellent appetite, did justice to the good cheer set before me.

The conversation, in the meantime, was spirited and general. The ladies, as usual, talked a great deal. I soon found that nearly all the company were well educated; and my host was a world of good-humored anecdote in himself. He seemed quite willing to speak of his position as superintendent of a *Maison de Santé*; and, indeed, the topic of lunacy was, much to my surprise, a favorite one with all present. A great many amusing stories were told, having reference to the *whims* of the patients.

"We had a fellow here once," said a fat little gentleman, who sat at my right,—"a fellow that fancied himself a teapot; and by the way, is it not especially singular how often this particular crotchet has entered the brain of the lunatic? There is scarcely an insane asylum in France which cannot supply a human teapot. *Our* gentleman was a Britannia-ware teapot, and was careful to polish himself every morning with buckskin and whiting."

"And then," said a tall man just opposite, "we had here, not long ago, a person who had taken it into his head that he was a donkey—which, allegorically speaking, you will say, was quite true. He was a troublesome patient; and we had much ado to keep him within bounds. For a long time he would eat nothing but thistles; but of this idea we soon cured him by insisting upon his eating nothing else. Then he was perpetually kicking out his heels—so—so—"

"Mr. De Kock! I will thank you to behave yourself!" here interrupted an old lady, who sat next to the speaker. "Please keep your feet to yourself! You have spoiled my brocade! Is it necessary, pray, to illustrate a remark in so practical a style? Our friend here can surely comprehend you without all this. Upon my word, you are nearly as great a donkey as the poor unfortunate imagined himself. Your acting is very natural, as I live."

"*Mille pardons! Ma'm'selle!*" replied Monsieur De Kock, thus addressed—

"a thousand pardons! I had no intention of offending. Ma'm'selle Laplace—Monsieur De Kock will do himself the honor of taking wine with you."

Here Monsieur De Kock bowed low, kissed his hand with much ceremony, and took wine with Ma'm'selle Laplace.

"Allow me, *mon ami*," now said Monsieur Maillard, addressing myself, "allow me to send you a morsel of this veal *à la St. Menhoult*—you will find it particularly fine."

At this instant three sturdy waiters had just succeeded in depositing safely upon the table an enormous dish, or trencher, containing what I supposed to be the "*monstrum, horrendum, informe, ingens, cui lumen ademptum.*" A closer scrutiny assured me, however, that it was only a small calf roasted whole, and set upon its knees, with an apple in its mouth, as is the English fashion of dressing a hare.

"Thank you, no," I replied; "to say the truth, I am not particularly partial to veal *à la St.*—what is it?—for I do not find that it altogether agrees with me. I will change my plate, however, and try some of the rabbit."

There were several side-dishes on the table, containing what appeared to be the ordinary French rabbit—a very delicious *morceau*, which I can recommend.

"Pierre," cried the host, "change this gentleman's plate, and give him a side-piece of this rabbit *au-chat*."

"This what?" said I.

"This rabbit *au-chat*."

"Why, thank you—upon second thoughts, no. I will just help myself to some of the ham."

There is no knowing what one eats, thought I to myself, at the tables of these people of the province. I will have none of their rabbit *au-chat*—and, for the matter of that, none of their *cat-au-rabbit* either.

"And then," said a cadaverous looking personage, near the foot of the table, taking up the thread of the conversation where it had been broken off,—"and then, among other oddities, we had a patient, once upon a time, who very pertinaciously maintained himself to be a Cordova cheese, and went about, with a knife in his hand, soliciting his friends to try a small slice from the middle of his leg."

"He was a great fool, beyond doubt," interposed some one, "but not to be compared with a certain individual whom we all know, with the exception of this strange gentleman. I mean the man who took himself for a bottle of champagne, and always went off with a pop and a fizz, in this fashion."

Here the speaker, very rudely, as I thought, put his right thumb in his left cheek, withdrew it with a sound resembling the popping of a cork, and then, by a dexterous movement of the tongue upon the teeth, created a sharp hissing and fizzing, which lasted for several minutes, in imitation of the frothing of champagne. This behavior, I saw plainly, was not very pleasing to Monsieur Maillard; but that gentleman said nothing, and the conversation was resumed by a very lean little man in a big wig.

"And then there was an ignoramus," said he, "who mistook himself for a frog; which, by the way, he resembled in no little degree. I wish you could have seen him, sir,"—here the speaker addressed myself,—"it would have done your heart good to see the natural airs that he put on. Sir, if that man was *not* a frog, I can only observe that it is a pity he was not. His croak thus—o-o-o-o-gh—o-o-o-o-gh! was the finest note in the world—B flat; and when he put his elbows upon the table thus—after taking a glass or two of wine—and distended his mouth, thus, and rolled up his eyes, thus, and winked them with excessive rapidity, thus, why then, sir, I take it upon myself to say, positively, that you would have been lost in admiration of the genius of the man."

"I have no doubt of it," I said.

"And then," said somebody else, "then there was Petit Gaillard, who thought himself a pinch of snuff, and was truly distressed because he could not take himself between his own finger and thumb."

"And then there was Jules Desoulières, who was a very singular genius, indeed, and went mad with the idea that he was a pumpkin. He persecuted the cook to make him up into pies—a thing which the cook indignantly refused to do. For my part, I am by no means sure that a pumpkin pie *à la Desoulières* would not have been very capital eating indeed!"

"You astonish me!" said I; and I looked inquisitively at Monsieur Maillard.

"Ha! ha! ha!" said that gentleman—"he! he! he!—hi! hi! hi!—ho! ho! ho!—hu! hu! hu! hu!—very good indeed! You must not be astonished, *mon ami*; our friend here is a wit—a *drôle*—you must not understand him to the letter."

"And then," said some other one of the party,—"then there was Bouffon Le Grand—another extraordinary personage in his way. He grew deranged through love, and fancied himself possessed of two heads. One of these he maintained to be the head of Cicero; the other he imagined a composite one, being Demosthenes' from the top of the forehead to the mouth, and Lord Brougham's from the mouth to the chin. It is not impossible that he was wrong; but he would have convinced you of his being in the right; for he was a man of great eloquence. He had an absolute passion for oratory, and could not refrain from display. For example, he used to leap upon the dinner-table thus, and—and—"

Here a friend, at the side of the speaker, put a hand upon his shoulder and whispered a few words in his ear: upon which he ceased talking with great suddenness, and sank back within his chair.

"And then," said the friend who had whispered, "there was Boullard, the tee-totum. I call him the tee-totum because, in fact, he was seized with the droll, but not altogether irrational, crotchet, that he had been converted into a tee-totum. You would have roared with laughter to see him spin. He would turn round upon one heel by the hour, in this manner—so—"

Here the friend whom he had just interrupted by a whisper, performed an exactly similar office for himself.

"But then," cried the old lady, at the top of her voice, "your Monsieur Boullard was a madman, and a very silly madman at best; for who, allow me to ask you, ever heard of a human tee-totum? The thing is absurd. Madame Joyeuse was a more sensible person, as you know. She had a crotchet, but it was instinct with common sense, and gave pleasure to all who had the honor of her acquaintance. She found, upon mature deliberation, that, by some accident, she had been turned into a chicken-cock; but, as such, she behaved with propriety. She flapped her wings with prodigious effect—so—so—and, as for her crow, it was delicious! Cock-a-doodle-doo!—cock-a-doodle-doo!—cock-a-doodle-de-doo dooo-do-o-o-o-o-o-o!"

"Madame Joyeuse, I will thank you to behave yourself!" here interrupted our host, very angrily. "You can either conduct yourself as a lady should do, or you can quit the table forthwith—take your choice."

The lady (whom I was much astonished to hear addressed as Madame Joyeuse, after the description of Madame Joyeuse she had just given) blushed up to the eyebrows, and seemed exceedingly abashed at the reproof. She hung down her head, and said not a syllable in reply. But another and younger lady resumed the theme. It was my beautiful girl of the little parlor.

"Oh, Madame Joyeuse *was* a fool!" she exclaimed, "but there was really much sound sense, after all, in the opinion of Eugénie Salsafette. She was a very beautiful and painfully modest young lady, who thought the ordinary mode of habiliment indecent, and wished to dress herself, always, by getting outside instead of inside of her clothes. It is a thing very easily done, after all. You have only to do so—and then so—so—so—and then so—so—so—and then—"

"Mon dieu! Ma'm'selle Salsafette!" here cried a dozen voices at once. "What *are* you about?—forbear!—that is sufficient!—we see, very plainly, how it is done!—hold! hold!" and several persons were already leaping from their seats to withhold Ma'm'selle Salsafette from putting herself upon a par with the Medicean Venus, when the point was very effectually and suddenly accomplished by a series of loud screams, or yells, from some portion of the main body of the *château*.

My nerves were very much affected, indeed, by these yells: but the rest of the company I really pitied. I never saw any set of reasonable people so thoroughly frightened in my life. They all grew as pale as so many corpses, and, shrinking within their seats, sat quivering and gibbering with terror, and listening for a repetition of the sound. It came again—louder and seemingly nearer—and then a third time *very* loud, and then a fourth time with a vigor evidently diminished. At this apparent dying away of the noise, the spirits of the company were immediately regained, and all was life and anecdote as before. I now ventured to inquire the cause of the disturbance.

"A mere *bagtelle*," said Monsieur Maillard. "We are used to these things, and care really very little about them. The lunatics, every now and then, get up a howl in concert; one starting another, as is sometimes the case with a bevy of dogs at night. It occasionally happens, however, that the *concerto* yells are succeeded by a simultaneous effort at breaking loose; when, of course, some little danger is to be apprehended."

"And how many have you in charge?"

"At present we have not more than ten, altogether."

"Principally females, I presume?"

"Oh, no—every one of them men, and stout fellows, too, I can tell you."

"Indeed! I have always understood that the majority of lunatics were of the gentler sex."

"It is generally so, but not always. Some time ago, there were about twenty-seven patients here; and, of that number, no less than eighteen were women; but, lately, matters have changed very much, as you see."

"Yes—have changed very much, as you see," here interrupted the gentleman who had broken the shins of Ma'm'selle Laplace.

"Yes—have changed very much, as you see!" chimed in the whole company at once.

"Hold your tongues, every one of you!" said my host, in a great rage. Where-upon the whole company maintained a dead silence for nearly a minute. As for one lady, she obeyed Monsieur Maillard to the letter, and thrusting out her tongue, which was an excessively long one, held it very resignedly, with both hands, until the end of the entertainment.

"And this gentlewoman," said I, to Monsieur Maillard, bending over and addressing him in a whisper—"this good lady who has just spoken, and who gives us the cock-a-doodle-de-doo—she, I presume, is harmless—quite harmless, eh?"

"Harmless!" ejaculated he, in unfeigned surprise, "why—why, what *can* you mean?"

"Only slightly touched?" said I, touching my head. "I take it for granted that she is not particularly—not dangerously affected, eh?"

"*Mon dieu!* what *is* it you imagine? This lady, my particular old friend, Madame Joyeuse, is as absolutely sane as myself. She has her little eccentricities, to be sure—but then, you know, all old women—all *very* old women—are more or less eccentric!"

"To be sure," said I,—"to be sure—and then the rest of these ladies and gentlemen—"

"Are my friends and keepers," interrupted Monsieur Maillard, drawing himself up with *hauteur*,—"my very good friends and assistants."

"What! all of them?" I asked,—"the women and all?"

"Assuredly," he said,—"we could not do at all without the women; they are the best lunatic nurses in the world; they have a way of their own, you know; their bright eyes have a marvellous effect—something like the fascination of the snake, you know."

"To be sure," said I,—"to be sure! They behave a little odd, eh?—they are a little *queer*, eh?—don't you think so?"

"Odd!—queer!—why, do you *really* think so? We are not very prudish, to be sure, here in the South—do pretty much as we please—enjoy life, and all that sort of thing, you know—"

"To be sure," said I,—"to be sure."

"And then, perhaps, this *Clos de Vougeôt* is a little heady, you know—a little *strong*—you understand, eh?"

"To be sure," said I,—"to be sure. By the by, Monsieur, did I understand you to say that the system you have adopted, in place of the celebrated soothing system, was one of very rigorous severity?"

"By no means. Our confinement is necessarily close; but the treatment—the medical treatment, I mean—is rather agreeable to the patients than otherwise."

"And the new system is one of your own invention?"

"Not altogether. Some portions of it are referable to Professor Tarr, of whom you have, necessarily, heard; and, again, there are modifications in my plan which I am happy to acknowledge as belonging of right to the celebrated Fether, with whom, if I mistake not, you have the honor of an intimate acquaintance."

"I am quite ashamed to confess," I replied, "that I have never even heard the names of either gentleman before."

"Good heavens!" ejaculated my host, drawing back his chair abruptly, and uplifting his hands. "I surely do not hear you aright! You did not intend to say, eh? that you had never *heard* either of the learned Doctor Tarr, or of the celebrated Professor Fether?"

"I am forced to acknowledge my ignorance," I replied; "but the truth should be held inviolate above all things. Nevertheless, I feel humbled to the dust, not to be acquainted with the works of these, no doubt, extraordinary men. I will seek out their writings forthwith, and peruse them with deliberate care. Monsieur Maillard, you have really—I must confess it—you have *really*—made me ashamed of myself!"

And this was the fact.

"Say no more, my good young friend," he said kindly, pressing my hand,— "join me now in a glass of Sauterne."

We drank. The company followed our example without stint. They chatted—they jested—they laughed—they perpetrated a thousand absurdities—the fiddles shrieked—the drum row-de-dowed—the trombones bellowed like so many brazen bulls of Phalaris—and the whole scene, growing gradually worse and worse, as the wines gained the ascendancy, became at length a sort of pandemonium *in petto*. In the meantime, Monsieur Maillard and myself, with some bottles of Sauterne and Vougeôt between us, continued our conversation at the top of the voice. A word spoken in an ordinary key stood no more chance of being heard than the voice of a fish from the bottom of Niagara Falls.

"And, sir," said I, screaming in his ear, "you mentioned something before dinner about the danger incurred in the old system of soothing. How is that?"

"Yes," he replied, "there was, occasionally, very great danger indeed. There is no accounting for the caprices of madmen; and, in my opinion as well as in that of Dr. Tarr and Professor Fether, it is *never* safe to permit them to run at large unattended. A lunatic may be 'soothed,' as it is called, for a time, but, in the end, he is very apt to become obstreperous. His cunning, too, is proverbial and great. If he has a project in view, he conceals his design with a marvellous wisdom; and the dexterity with which he counterfeits sanity, presents, to the metaphysician, one of the most singular problems in the study of mind. When a madman appears *thoroughly* sane, indeed, it is high time to put him in a straitjacket."

"But the *danger*, my dear sir, of which you were speaking—in your own experience—during your control of this house—have you had practical reason to think liberty hazardous in the case of a lunatic?"

"Here?—in my own experience?—why, I may say, yes. For example:—no *very* long while ago, a singular circumstance occurred in this very house. The 'soothing system,' you know, was then in operation, and the patients were at large.

They behaved remarkably well—especially so,—any one of sense might have known that some devilish scheme was brewing from that particular fact, that the fellows behaved so *remarkably* well. And, sure enough, one fine morning the keepers found themselves pinioned hand and foot, and thrown into the cells, where they were attended, as if *they* were the lunatics, by the lunatics themselves, who had usurped the offices of the keepers."

"You don't tell me so! I never heard of any thing so absurd in my life!"

"Fact—it all came to pass by means of a stupid fellow—a lunatic—who, by some means, had taken it into his head that he had invented a better system of government than any ever heard of before—of lunatic government, I mean. He wished to give his invention a trial, I suppose, and so he persuaded the rest of the patients to join him in a conspiracy for the overthrow of the reigning powers."

"And he really succeeded?"

"No doubt of it. The keepers and kept were soon made to exchange places. Not that exactly either, for the madmen had been free, but the keepers were shut up in cells forthwith, and treated, I am sorry to say, in a very cavalier manner."

"But I presume a counter-revolution was soon effected. This condition of things could not have long existed. The country people in the neighborhood— visitors coming to see the establishment—would have given the alarm."

"There you are out. The head rebel was too cunning for that. He admitted no visitors at all—with the exception, one day, of a very stupid-looking young gentleman of whom he had no reason to be afraid. He let him in to see the place—just by way of variety,—to have a little fun with him. As soon as he had gammoned him sufficiently, he let him out, and sent him about his business."

"And *how* long, then, did the madmen reign?"

"Oh, a very long time, indeed—a month certainly—how much longer I can't precisely say. In the meantime, the lunatics had a jolly season of it—that you may swear. They doffed their own shabby clothes, and made free with the family wardrobe and jewels. The cellars of the *château* were well stocked with wine; and these madmen are just the devils that know how to drink it. They lived well, I can tell you."

"And the treatment—what was the particular species of treatment which the leader of the rebels put into operation?"

"Why, as for that, a madman is not necessarily a fool, as I have already observed; and it is my honest opinion that his treatment was a much better treatment than that which it superseded. It was a very capital system indeed—simple—neat—no trouble at all—in fact it was delicious—it was—"

Here my host's observations were cut short by another series of yells, of the same character as those which had previously disconcerted us. This time, however, they seemed to proceed from persons rapidly approaching.

"Gracious heavens!" I ejaculated—"the lunatics have most undoubtedly broken loose."

"I very much fear it is so," replied Monsieur Maillard, now becoming excessively pale. He had scarcely finished the sentence, before loud shouts and imprecations were heard beneath the windows; and, immediately afterward, it became evident that some persons outside were endeavoring to gain entrance into the room. The door was beaten with what appeared to be a sledge-hammer, and the shutters were wrenched and shaken with prodigious violence.

A scene of the most terrible confusion ensued. Monsieur Maillard, to my excessive astonishment, threw himself under the sideboard. I had expected more resolution at his hands. The members of the orchestra, who, for the last fifteen minutes, had been seemingly too much intoxicated to do duty, now sprang all at once to their feet and to their instruments, and, scrambling upon their table, broke out, with one accord, into, "Yankee Doodle," which they performed, if not exactly in tune, at least with an energy superhuman, during the whole of the uproar.

Meantime, upon the main dining-table, among the bottles and glasses,

leaped the gentleman who, with such difficulty, had been restrained from leaping there before. As soon as he fairly settled himself, he commenced an oration, which, no doubt, was a very capital one, if it could only have been heard. At the same moment, the man with the tee-totum predilection, set himself to spinning around the apartment, with immense energy, and with arms outstretched at right angles with his body; so that he had all the air of a tee-to-tum in fact, and knocked everybody down that happened to get in his way. And now, too, hearing an incredible popping and fizzing of champagne, I discovered at length, that it proceeded from the person who performed the bottle of that delicate drink during dinner. And then, again, the frog-man croaked away as if the salvation of his soul depended upon every note that he uttered. And, in the midst of all this, the continuous braying of a donkey arose over all. As for my old friend, Madame Joyeuse, I really could have wept for the poor lady, she appeared so terribly perplexed. All she did, however, was to stand up in a corner, by the fireplace, and sing out incessantly at the top of her voice, "Cock-a-doodle-de-dooooooh!"

And now came the climax—the catastrophe of the drama. As no resistance, beyond whooping and yelling and cock-a-doodling, was offered to the encroachments of the party without, the ten windows were very speedily, and almost simultaneously, broken in. But I shall never forget the emotions of wonder and horror with which I gazed, when, leaping through these windows, and down among us *pêle-mêle*, fighting, stamping, scratching, and howling, there rushed a perfect army of what I took to be Chimpanzees, ourang-outangs, or big black baboons of the Cape of Good Hope.

I received a terrible beating—after which I rolled under a sofa and lay still. After lying there some fifteen minutes, however, during which time I listened with all my ears to what was going on in the room, I came to some satisfactory *dénouement* of this tragedy. Monsieur Maillard, it appeared, in giving me the account of the lunatic who had excited his fellows to rebellion, had been merely relating his own exploits. This gentleman had, indeed, some two or three years before, been the superintendent of the establishment; but grew crazy himself, and so became a patient. This fact was unknown to the travelling companion who introduced me. The keepers, ten in number, having been suddenly over-powered, were first well tarred, then carefully feathered, and then shut up in underground cells. They had been so imprisoned for more than a month, during which period Monsieur Maillard had generously allowed them not only the tar and feathers (which constituted his "system"), but some bread and abundance of water. The latter was pumped on them daily. At length, one escaping through a sewer, gave freedom to all the rest.

The "soothing system," with important modifications, has been resumed at the *château*; yet I cannot help agreeing with Monsieur Maillard, that his own "treatment" was a very capital one of its kind. As he justly observed, it was "simple—neat—and gave no trouble at all—not the least."

I have only to add that, although I have searched every library in Europe for the works of Doctor *Tarr* and Professor *Fether*, I have, up to the present day, utterly failed in my endeavors to procure a copy.

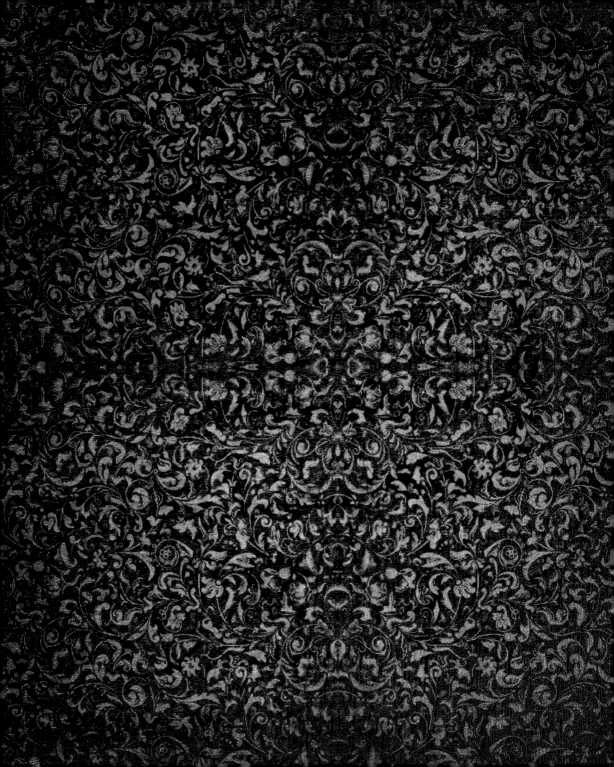

11. POEMS

The Raven

Once upon a midnight dreary, while I pondered, weak and weary,
Over many a quaint and curious volume of forgotten lore—
While I nodded, nearly napping, suddenly there came a tapping,
As of some one gently rapping, rapping at my chamber door.
"'Tis some visitor," I muttered, "tapping at my chamber door—
Only this and nothing more."

Ah, distinctly I remember it was in the bleak December,
And each separate dying ember wrought its ghost upon the floor.
Eagerly I wished the morrow;—vainly I had sought to borrow
From my books surcease of sorrow—sorrow for the lost Lenore—
For the rare and radiant maiden whom the angels name Lenore—
Nameless here for evermore.

And the silken sad uncertain rustling of each purple curtain
Thrilled me—filled me with fantastic terrors never felt before;
So that now, to still the beating of my heart, I stood repeating:
"'Tis some visitor entreating entrance at my chamber door—
Some late visitor entreating entrance at my chamber door;
This it is, and nothing more."

Presently my soul grew stronger; hesitating then no longer,
"Sir," said I, "or Madam, truly your forgiveness I implore;
But the fact is I was napping, and so gently you came rapping,
And so faintly you came tapping, tapping at my chamber door,
That I scarce was sure I heard you"—here I opened wide the door;—
Darkness there and nothing more.

Deep into that darkness peering, long I stood there wondering, fearing,
Doubting, dreaming dreams no mortals ever dared to dream before;
But the silence was unbroken, and the stillness gave no token,
And the only word there spoken was the whispered word, "Lenore!"
This I whispered, and an echo murmured back the word, "Lenore!"—
Merely this and nothing more.

Back into the chamber turning, all my soul within me burning,
Soon again I heard a tapping something louder than before.
"Surely," said I, "surely that is something at my window lattice;
Let me see, then, what thereat is, and this mystery explore—
Let my heart be still a moment, and this mystery explore;—
'Tis the wind and nothing more."

Open here I flung the shutter, when, with many a flirt and flutter,
In there stepped a stately Raven of the saintly days of yore.
Not the least obeisance made he; not an instant stopped or stayed he,
But, with mien of lord or lady, perched above my chamber door—
Perched upon a bust of Pallas just above my chamber door—
Perched, and sat, and nothing more.

Then this ebony bird beguiling my sad fancy into smiling,
By the grave and stern decorum of the countenance it wore,
"Though thy crest be shorn and shaven, thou," I said, "art sure no craven,
Ghastly grim and ancient Raven wandering from the Nightly shore—
Tell me what thy lordly name is on the Night's Plutonian shore!"
Quoth the Raven, "Nevermore."

Much I marvelled this ungainly fowl to hear discourse so plainly,
Though its answer little meaning—little relevancy bore;
For we cannot help agreeing that no living human being
Ever yet was blessed with seeing bird above his chamber door—
Bird or beast upon the sculptured bust above his chamber door,
With such name as "Nevermore."

But the Raven, sitting lonely on the placid bust, spoke only
That one word, as if his soul in that one word he did outpour.
Nothing farther then he uttered; not a feather then he fluttered—
Till I scarcely more than muttered: "Other friends have flown before—
On the morrow *he* will leave me as my hopes have flown before."
Then the bird said, "Nevermore."

Startled at the stillness broken by reply so aptly spoken,
"Doubtless," said I, "what it utters is its only stock and store,
Caught from some unhappy master whom unmerciful Disaster
Followed fast and followed faster till his songs one burden bore—
Till the dirges of his Hope that melancholy burden bore
Of 'Never—nevermore.'"

But the Raven still beguiling all my sad soul into smiling,
Straight I wheeled a cushioned seat in front of bird and bust and door;
Then, upon the velvet sinking, I betook myself to linking
Fancy unto fancy, thinking what this ominous bird of yore—
What this grim, ungainly, ghastly, gaunt, and ominous bird of yore
Meant in croaking "Nevermore."

This I sat engaged in guessing, but no syllable expressing
To the fowl whose fiery eyes now burned into my bosom's core;
This and more I sat divining, with my head at ease reclining
On the cushion's velvet lining that the lamp-light gloated o'er,
But whose velvet violet lining with the lamp-light gloating o'er
She shall press, ah, nevermore!

Then, methought, the air grew denser, perfumed from an unseen censer
Swung by Seraphim whose foot-falls tinkled on the tufted floor.
"Wretch," I cried, "thy God hath lent thee—by these angels he hath sent thee
Respite—respite and nepenthe from thy memories of Lenore!
Quaff, oh quaff this kind nepenthe and forget this lost Lenore!"
Quoth the Raven, "Nevermore."

"Prophet!" said I, "thing of evil!—prophet still, if bird or devil!—
Whether Tempter sent, or whether tempest tossed thee here ashore,
Desolate yet all undaunted, on this desert land enchanted—
On this home by Horror haunted,—tell me truly, I implore—
Is there—*is* there balm in Gilead?—tell me—tell me, I implore!"
Quoth the Raven, "Nevermore."

"Prophet!" said I, "thing of evil—prophet still, if bird or devil!
By that heaven that bends above us—by that God we both adore—
Tell this soul with sorrow laden if, within the distant Aidenn,
It shall clasp a sainted maiden whom the angels name Lenore—
Clasp a rare and radiant maiden whom the angels name Lenore."
Quoth the Raven, "Nevermore."

"Be that word our sign of parting, bird or fiend!" I shrieked, upstarting—
"Get thee back into the tempest and the Night's Plutonian shore!
Leave no black plume as a token of that lie thy soul hath spoken!
Leave my loneliness unbroken!—quit the bust above my door!
Take thy beak from out my heart, and take thy form from off my door!"
Quoth the Raven, "Nevermore."

And the Raven, never flitting, still is sitting, still is sitting
On the pallid bust of Pallas just above my chamber door;
And his eyes have all the seeming of a demon's that is dreaming,
And the lamp-light o'er him streaming throws his shadow on the floor;
And my soul from out that shadow that lies floating on the floor
Shall be lifted—nevermore!

To Helen

I saw thee once—once only—years ago;
I must not say *how* many—but *not* many.
It was a July midnight; and from out
A full-orbed moon, that, like thine own soul, soaring,
Sought a precipitate pathway up through heaven,
There fell a silvery-silken veil of light,
With quietude, and sultriness, and slumber,
Upon the upturned faces of a thousand
Roses that grew in an enchanted garden,
Where no wind dared to stir, unless on tiptoe—
Fell on the upturn'd faces of these roses
That gave out, in return for the love-light,
Their odorous souls in an ecstatic death—
Fell on the upturn'd faces of these roses
That smiled and died in this parterre, enchanted
By thee, and by the poetry of thy presence.

Clad all in white, upon a violet bank
I saw thee half reclining; while the moon
Fell on the upturn'd faces of the roses,
And on thine own, upturn'd—alas, in sorrow!
Was it not Fate that, on this July midnight—
Was it not Fate (whose name is also Sorrow),
That bade me pause before that garden-gate,
To breathe the incense of those slumbering roses?
No footstep stirred; the hated world all slept,
Save only thee and me. (Oh, Heaven!—oh, God!
How my heart beats in coupling those two words!)
Save only thee and me. I paused—I looked—
And in an instant all things disappeared.
(Ah, bear in mind this garden was enchanted!)

The pearly lustre of the moon went out;
The mossy banks and the meandering paths,
The happy flowers and the repining trees,
Were seen no more: the very roses' odors
Died in the arms of the adoring airs.
All—all expired save thee—save less than thou:
Save only the divine light in thine eyes—
Save but the soul in thine uplifted eyes.
I saw but them—they were the world to me.
I saw but them—saw only them for hours—
Saw only them until the moon went down.
What wild heart-histories seemed to lie enwritten
Upon those crystalline, celestial spheres!

How dark a woe! yet how sublime a hope!
How silently serene a sea of pride!
How daring an ambition! yet how deep—
How fathomless a capacity for love!
But now, at length, dear Dian sank from sight,
Into a western couch of thunder-cloud;
And thou, a ghost, amid the entombing trees
Didst glide away. *Only thine eyes remained.*
They *would not* go—they never yet have gone.
Lighting my lonely pathway home that night,
They have not left me (as my hopes have) since.

They follow me—they lead me through the years.
They are my ministers—yet I their slave.
Their office is to illumine and enkindle—
My duty, *to be saved* by their bright light,
And purified in their electric fire,
And sanctified in their Elysian fire.
They fill my soul with Beauty (which is Hope),
And are far up in heaven—the stars I kneel to
In the sad, silent watches of my night;
While even in the meridian glare of day
I see them still—two sweetly scintillant
Venuses, unextinguished by the sun!

The City in the Sea

Lo! Death has reared himself a throne
In a strange city lying alone
Far down within the dim West
Where the good and the bad and the worst and the best
Have gone to their eternal rest.
There shrines and palaces and towers
(Time-eaten towers that tremble not!)
Resemble nothing that is ours.
Around, by lifting winds forgot,
Resignedly beneath the sky
The melancholy waters lie.

No rays from the holy Heaven come down
On the long night-time of that town;
But light from out the lurid sea
Streams up the turrets silently—
Gleams up the pinnacles far and free—
Up domes—up spires—up kingly halls—
Up fanes—up Babylon-like walls—
Up shadowy long-forgotten bowers
Of sculptured ivy and stone flowers—
Up many and many a marvellous shrine
Whose wreathèd friezes intertwine
The viol, the violet, and the vine.

Resignedly beneath the sky
The melancholy waters lie.
So blend the turrets and shadows there
That all seem pendulous in air,
While from a proud tower in the town
Death looks gigantically down.

There open fanes and gaping graves
Yawn level with the luminous waves;
But not the riches there that lie
In each idol's diamond eye—
Not the gaily-jewelled dead
Tempt the waters from their bed;
For no ripples curl, alas!
Along that wilderness of glass—
No swellings tell that winds may be
Upon some far-off happier sea—
No heavings hint that winds have been
On seas less hideously serene.

But lo, a stir is in the air!
The wave—there is a movement there!
As if the towers had thrown aside,
In slightly sinking, the dull tide—
As if their tops had feebly given
A void within the filmy Heaven.
The waves have now a redder glow—
The hours are breathing faint and low—
And when, amid no earthly moans,
Down, down that town shall settle hence,
Hell, rising from a thousand thrones,
Shall do it reverence.

A Dream
Within a Dream

Take this kiss upon the brow!
And, in parting from you now,
Thus much let me avow—
You are not wrong, who deem
That my days have been a dream;
Yet if hope has flown away
In a night, or in a day,
In a vision, or in none,
Is it therefore the less *gone*?
All that we see or seem
Is but a dream within a dream.

I stand amid the roar
Of a surf-tormented shore,
And I hold within my hand
Grains of the golden sand—
How few! yet how they creep
Through my fingers to the deep,
While I weep—while I weep!
O God! can I not grasp
Them with a tighter clasp?
O God! can I not save
One from the pitiless wave?
Is *all* that we see or seem
But a dream within a dream?

The Conqueror Worm

LO! t'is a gala night
    Within the lonesome latter years!
An angel throng, bewinged, bedight
    In veils, and drowned in tears,
Sit in a theatre, to see
    A play of hopes and fears,
While the orchestra breathes fitfully
    The music of the spheres.

Mimes, in the form of God on high,
    Mutter and mumble low,
And hither and thither fly—
    Mere puppets they, who come and go
At bidding of vast formless things
    That shift the scenery to and fro,
Flapping from out their Condor wings
    Invisible Woe!

That motley drama—oh, be sure
    It shall not be forgot!
With its Phantom chased for evermore,
    By a crowd that seize it not,
Through a circle that ever returneth in
    To the self-same spot,
And much of Madness, and more of Sin,
    And Horror the soul of the plot.

But see, amid the mimic rout
    A crawling shape intrude!
A blood-red thing that writhes from out
    The scenic solitude!
It writhes!—it writhes!—with mortal pangs
    The mimes become its food,
And the angels sob at vermin fangs
    In human gore imbued.

Out—out are the lights—out all!
    And, over each quivering form,
The curtain, a funeral pall,
    Comes down with the rush of a storm,
And the angels, all pallid and wan,
    Uprising, unveiling, affirm
That the play is the tragedy "Man,"
    And its hero the Conqueror Worm.

The Bells

I.

Hear the sledges with the bells—
Silver bells!
What a world of merriment their melody foretells!
How they tinkle, tinkle, tinkle,
In the icy air of night!
While the stars that oversprinkle
All the heavens seem to twinkle
With a crystalline delight;
Keeping time, time, time,
In a sort of Runic rhyme,
To the tintinabulation that so musically wells
From the bells, bells, bells, bells,
Bells, bells, bells—
From the jingling and the tinkling of the bells.

II.

Hear the mellow wedding bells,
Golden bells!
What a world of happiness their harmony foretells!
Through the balmy air of night

How they ring out their delight!
    From the molten-golden notes,
    And all in tune,
    What a liquid ditty floats
To the turtle-dove that listens, while she gloats
    On the moon!
    Oh, from out the sounding cells
What a gush of euphony voluminously wells!
    How it swells!
    How it dwells
    On the Future! how it tells
    Of the rapture that impels
To the swinging and the ringing
    Of the bells, bells, bells,
Of the bells, bells, bells, bells,
    Bells, bells, bells—
To the rhyming and the chiming of the bells!

III.

Hear the loud alarum bells—
    Brazen bells!
What a tale of terror, now, their turbulency tells!
    In the startled ear of night
    How they scream out their affright!
    Too much horrified to speak,
    They can only shriek, shriek,
    Out of tune,

In a clamorous appealing to the mercy of the fire,
In a mad expostulation with the deaf and frantic fire,
 Leaping higher, higher, higher,
 With a desperate desire,
 And a resolute endeavor
 Now—now to sit, or never,
 By the side of the pale-faced moon
 Oh, the bells, bells, bells!
 What a tale their terror tells
  Of despair!
 How they clang, and clash, and roar!
 What a horror they outpour
On the bosom of the palpitating air!
 Yet the ear it fully knows,
  By the twanging,
  And the clanging,
 How the danger ebbs and flows;
 Yet the ear distinctly tells,
  In the jangling,
  And the wrangling,
 How the danger sinks and swells,
By the sinking or the swelling in the anger of the bells—
  Of the bells—
 Of the bells, bells, bells, bells,
  Bells, bells, bells—
In the clamour and the clangor of the bells!

IV.

Hear the tolling of the bells—
Iron bells!
What a world of solemn thought their monody compels!
In the silence of the night,
How we shiver with affright
At the melancholy meaning of their tone!
For every sound that floats
From the rust within their throats
Is a groan.
And the people—ah, the people—
They that dwell up in the steeple,
All alone,
And who tolling, tolling, tolling,
In that muffled monotone,
Feel a glory in so rolling
On the human heart a stone—
They are neither man nor woman—
They are neither brute nor human—
They are Ghouls:
And their king it is who tolls;
And he rolls, rolls, rolls,
Rolls
A pæan from the bells!

And his merry bosom swells
     With the pæan of the bells!
And he dances, and he yells;
Keeping time, time, time,
In a sort of Runic rhyme,
     To the pæan of the bells—
          Of the bells:
Keeping time, time, time,
In a sort of Runic rhyme,
     To the throbbing of the bells—
Of the bells, bells, bells—
     To the sobbing of the bells;
Keeping time, time, time,
     As he knells, knells, knells,
In a happy Runic rhyme,
     To the rolling of the bells—
Of the bells, bells, bells—
     To the tolling of the bells,
Of the bells, bells, bells, bells—
          Bells, bells, bells—
To the moaning and the groaning of the bells.